FLORENCE

Pamela K Carter

3P
PUBLISHING

Copyright © 3P Publishing
First published in 2022 in the UK

3P Publishing
C E C, London Road Corby
NN17 5EU

A catalogue number for this book is available from
the British Library

ISBN: 978-1-913740-35-1

Cover design: James Mossop

Dedicated to the memory
of Elizabeth Oddie,
my teacher at The Green School
who terrified me, yet inspired me
to love the English language.

Contents

Preface

Last night, my sisters kept teasing me. Well, they often do that. Living with four of them and another four uncouth brothers often causes friction. Even though I love them to bits, they never afford me any privacy. Lizzie and I share a bed with Harriet and when the candle is finally blown out, we lie snug in the darkness and our whispers turn to giggles and inevitable teasing. Sometimes I wonder how we all fit into this thatched cottage - and it's really only one third of the building as we share it with two other families - but Ma still has nine of us at home. My brothers sleep downstairs, whilst us five girls squeeze into an attic beneath the straw roof, but not for much longer.

I know something they don't know.

Harriet is sniffing.

"Flo! You stink of onions, gal! I wouldn't want your smelly job. Does the old boy keep you permanently pickling in the kitchen?"

This suggestive comment elicits giggles from everyone. I protest with a loud "No!"

Then I calmly say, "I have all sorts of jobs to do, and anyway, he's not that old."

Our oldest sister Sue calls out from her truckle bed. "You won't get me going into service; too much like slavery!"

I'm ready to retaliate. "Yes, but you've got smelly cows to milk every day and we all know why you are so keen on that!"

"George!" we all chorus together, knowing she's got her eye on the farmer's son.

Father's voice bellows sternly from below. "Girls! Quiet up there!"

Lizzie wriggles closer and finds my hand, which she clasps tight. "Is it that bad up at the vicarage?" she whispers.

I have to think hard before answering. I haven't the heart to tell them what is really happening. I hesitate before saying quickly, "The Reverend is very kind to me. His wife died some years ago and he needs help, so I have to do all sorts of things. The worst job is clearing out the massive grate, which is always messy to do. I hate that!"

What I can't say is how good he is to me, as I'm aware my siblings have far more menial, boring and repetitive jobs either on the farm, in the village laundry or at the local shoe factory. You see, my Reverend is a very kindly Welshman. He's very proper in his ways and respected in his church. I'd been there about six weeks when he asked me into his study and fired many questions at me, which I answered as best I could. I got quite a shock as one of them was in French, but I sort of knew what he was asking, because my grandmother had a smattering of the old language from her Huguenot ancestors and I think the Reverend was quite surprised when I replied with the few words I knew, and then I got the surprise of my life!

Chapter 1
July

There's nothing better than strolling along a country lane on a fine, warm July morning, with the sound of the bees as they settle on the remnants of hawthorn blossom or nestle down on the wild plants that scatter along the edge of the lane. I finally feel at peace on my half-day off, away from the confines of home life, and have escaped on the pretext of visiting Great Aunt Sarah. I need time to think about what has been suggested, for in my heart I sense it could be the start of something way beyond my capabilities. Father had always given me encouragement to work hard when I was in school. He seemed to recognise that I had the ability to learn fast.

He used to say, "You try and get on in this hard old life. Better yourself, our Flo. Work hard and you'll be rewarded by the good Lord."

So now, with those words spinning in my head, I must choose my path in life.

A brown partridge suddenly shoots out from beneath a thorny bush and startles me with its stuttering cry and its very action jolts me into thinking straight. I go over the scene back in the Reverend's study. It had all seemed so natural to respond to him when he spoke to me in French and now, I begin to wonder why he did that. Maybe he'd overhead me as I was preparing meals in the kitchen, for I know I have a habit of singing some little rhymes that we were taught as children like the jolly sound of 'Lundi Matin' or that old favourite 'Frère Jacques'. I find it helps pass the time and I know that Miss Ophelia sometimes is outside door and she listens in, because

I hear her skirts swish as she returns to her room, and I know she goes off humming those little tunes.

I was only employed at the vicarage two months ago on the understanding that I was to cook a lunchtime meal for Reverend Henderson and his only daughter, and do any other kitchen jobs required. I would be assisted by a village girl Millie for the general jobs around the house. She's a bundle of nerves and rather prone to knocking things over, added to which she made such a mess when she first tried to clear the fire grate that I felt it wiser just to take on that onerous task myself until she was properly trained. The nicest thing about working here is that we are rarely observed, and no one is breathing down our necks or chastening us for work not done in time. I still feel there's a lot to learn, but I feel fortunate to have secured this position. So why does the guilt of my pleasure weigh so heavily upon me? It thrilled me the other day when the Reverend spoke to me and said some very complimentary things about me.

"You are a very intelligent girl, young Florence, and I feel you have settled here in your job most satisfactorily. You been a great help to both myself and my daughter. She still misses her dear mother, and needs time to grieve her untimely passing. With your presence, I feel Ophelia has begun to emerge from the darkness."

I felt in awe as the Reverend stood and held his well-worn bible high in the air and his voice thundered out aloud.

"For you were formerly darkness, but now you are the light in the Lord; walk as children of light!"

I confess I had no clue as to where that quotation came from. Was he referring to me as a child of the light? Maybe he was testing me to prove I was worthy? Following that outburst, I felt extremely nervous, but then in softer tones he continued:

"Ophelia tells me she has taken a liking to having you in our home, so much so that I want to offer you the position of companion to my daughter. It would give us both great pleasure if you would consider becoming part of our family."

4

I must have stood there with a look of disbelief upon my face as I contemplated the suggestion, lost for words, but with a growing sense of importance and pride. The warm feeling I experienced when he addresses me as Florence is uppermost in my thoughts. If I turned this offer down, I might possibly be asked to leave this employment and what shame that would bring upon my dear family. Yet that one simple act had such a powerful effect on me that I was impelled to reply. "Thank you, Reverend Henderson. If I can help you in that way, I will."

Miss Ophelia must have been listening nearby for she suddenly burst into her father's study, smiled broadly at me and then threw her arms around his neck. I had to suppress a chuckle as his spiritual demeanour evaporated and I noticed his eyes mellow with a warmth of affection towards his impulsive daughter.

"Go on! Shoo, both of you! No disturbing me now, as I've sermons to write."

I retreated with the excuse I needed to finish preparing a meal, but headed for the makeshift wooden seat just by the vicarage wall overlooking the circular rose bed that the late Mrs Henderson had created. In the warm July air, I was calmed by the fragrant scents that wafted over me. Had I actually said I would agree to the Reverend's request? My strengths lay in my ability to cook, so what did I know about being a companion? However, the more I thought about it, the more attractive the proposition became.

And that is why I needed that moment of solitude to make things clear in my head. Watching the white clouds tumble and shift overhead I resolved to make the most of this golden opportunity, so my biggest dilemma was facing how my family will react. How could I tell my sisters that my position at the vicarage was not one of merely slaving over a hot stove, but was to be more of a companion to his lonely daughter, the young Miss Henderson?

She had approached me last week as I was gathering some thyme and fresh mint from just outside the kitchen doorway, and as she stood there, looking a trifle hesitant and very nervous, I observed her patting her palms together as if she was deciding what to say.

"Hello. You don't mind me watching you, do you? It's so good to be out in the fresh air."

There followed an uneasy silence, but when I smiled at her she beamed back at me and gently laid her hand on my arm in a gesture of friendship.

"I do love your dark hair, Flo. Mine is so unruly because of all these curls. Mama used to brush it for me several times a day. Oh, I do miss her." Her bottom lip quivered, but she composed herself, continuing, "You don't mind if I talk with you, do you? I'd very much like to be best friends with you and I hope you don't mind me calling you Florence. That a sweet name! Mr Dennison has been a strict taskmaster today and I simply hate having to be in that stuffy room for my tedious piano lessons when it's so warm outside."

"Oh, Miss Ophelia, you play so well."

I'd heard her playing and was in awe, as it sounded perfect to my ears and I'd always imagined it gave her great pleasure to play. Once when I knew that both she and her father were out on a morning's visit, I had the temerity to let my hands feel the imposing black and white keyboard, becoming quite enchanted as various notes rang out. Their resonance seemed to shatter the stillness in the house and I guiltily returned to my kitchen work.

Now, as we stood together, a large magpie suddenly dropped to the path and eyed us both before pecking in the nearby borders. Instinctively I went on alert, remembering that ancient saying, "One for sorrow", but that moment evaporated as a second magpie flew down to join the other. I seem to recall that both of us laughed out aloud and chanted together, "Two for joy!"

I think it was at that moment I knew things would work out for us both, although I could foresee a demanding time ahead.

6

Chapter 2
Higher Weldon

As you approach Higher Weldon there is a strange mound on the left of the road with an overgrown ditch full of brambles, with just one area trampled to the side where the young lads from the village dare each other to run up to the top without stopping. The residents take great pride in this historical mound, as legend goes there once being a Norman castle upon its summit.

There are now only a handful of run-down cottages that straggle the side of the twisting, running brook. Many are in desperate need of a new thatch, others missing window panes which are covered with rags to stop the biting winter winds that cut across the land. They are the homes of the farm workers, those that are anchored to their menial tasks without thought of ever bettering themselves. The land all around is parcelled into irregular fields for growing the corn, or for vital sugar beet to feed the cattle. The hedgerows that form the boundaries are like little sanctuaries, where the children of the village hide from the raw winds while they gather the wild berries and nettles and anything else they can glean from the edge of the field. In those rare moments when I am not working, I love nothing better than to wander alone through the quaint country lanes, absorbing the smells of the undergrowth, or freshly cut grass whilst listening to the incessant sparrow chatter as they flit among the hedges.

My baby sister Mary and her two friends Evie and May have to walk these lanes on their way back from the bigger village of Lower Weldon after their school classes each day. They often choose the route across the fields and along by the

7

hedges rather than the longer, winding dirt track which is rutted with cart wheels and churned up by the noisy farm vehicles that are so unpopular with the workers.

"I hate Miss Cross! She really hurt me!" May is rubbing her knuckles, and still feeling mad that she'd been caught out whispering across her wooden desk.

"Cross Patch! Cross Patch! She can scratch! She can scratch!" chant her two friends with grins on their faces. They know that almost every school attendee has a private nickname for their strict dictatorial head teacher with that relevant name.

Evie starts to giggle. "Why do we have to learn all about being 'conkered'? Do conkers get thrown at you 'til you die?"

Mary throws her head back and chuckles. "Oh, you are a goose, Evie! It doesn't mean conkers! This French King sailed with his armies and he conquered us when he won this famous battle. So he's our King now, well not now, 'cos we've got a Queen. Come on! Race you to the brook!" She charges ahead in such a rush that her foot gets caught on one of the roots and ends up flat on her face. Evie is fast behind her with that permanent worried look upon her pallid face.

"You all right, Mary? Oh gosh, your nose is cut." She pulls a crumpled rag from her sleeve and starts to wipe the blood away as Mary sits back against the base of a hawthorn bush. "It's not too bad." May helps her friend to her feet, brushing the odd flecks of dirt and leaves mainly from her pinafore.

"I'll come with you Mary, and we can tell your ma it was just a trip and you hadn't been fighting with the boys again."

The three friends walk steadily towards the opening in the corner of the field where they have to leap over the brook and onto the road. May heads one way whilst Evie hangs on to Mary's arm and they turn towards one of the cottages.

I was getting anxious that Mary was later than usual and could sense Ma fretting as she repeatedly glanced out of the kitchen window. Ma is still very strict about all of the family eating together of an evening. Woe betide any of the boys who have not washed their hands, or they will feel the sharpness of their mother's own hand across their ears. I can see her sense of relief when Mary finally slinks into the room, although Ma is tight lipped as she notices the unkempt hair and bloody nose. All she does is to haul Mary over to the corner sink and roughly clean the graze with cold water.

"I tripped and fell, Ma, and that's the honest truth."

Ma gives her a harsh, quizzical look as if in disbelief but still says nothing. Mary sits next to me on her little stool as she knows I will not pry or condemn her. She slips her sticky hand in mine and I squeeze it to reassure her as we exchange a comforting smile.

"I really did trip our Flo; I wasn't fighting this time!"

She's trying to ignore the throbbing pain in her nose and keeps her head down in the vague hope Jack won't be teasing her about the fall. I can see how sore it looks so bend low and whisper, "I believe you. Is it very sore? I promise when we have eaten, I'll put some salve on to soothe the rawness."

I look at her concerned face and wonder what is going on inside her troubled head as she bites the nail of her thumb. Then as Ma hands round our plates there is a brief moment of silence as everyone tucks into their meal. I am still trying to summon up the courage to tell my family about the changes that have taken place at the vicarage, but now is not the right time.

Mary is frowning as she eats and I sense she is tossing something over in her mind for she keeps glancing up at me as if wanting to question me but dare not do so.

In fact, Mary idolises her elder sister but she senses Flo is hiding something. She, unlike her siblings, notices that Flo doesn't laugh as much as before and she can tell from the slightly worried look that things aren't normal. Mary is of an age when she even begins to wonder if Flo is in the family way. She listens to the tales her sisters regale of a night-time about their friends who get caught. Mary isn't quite sure what this really means, but knows it involves boys. Well, she's aware of a nice lad with ginger hair that hangs around outside, leaning on his bicycle with a dreamy look on his face when Flo passes by and she notices how little Flo eats at mealtimes, always with her excuses that her brothers need more food than she does.

"So, what did the old Cross Patch teach you today, our Mary? Does she still make you chant out the nine times table? Fat lot of use that was!"

"Hold your tongue, Joe! Stop teasing our Mary!"

Dad glares at the faces around the table. He has a very soft spot for this last living child who brightens the end of his day with her happy smiles and little stories about her friends in nearby villages. Thankfully he seems unaware of her marked nose.

"It wasn't Miss Cross all day Pa; some gentleman visited us and he showed us pictures of great stone castles and told us all about William the Conqueror and I put my hand up and said we once had a castle in our village. Then he tells us that ours would have been a wooden one when they were first done, not massive stones."

Jack giggles when he thinks of the times he and his mates spent looking for the crumbled stone ruins that were rumoured to be scatted down in the derelict moat. "You can't have a wooden castle and you know why? "Cos it wouldn't stand up!" He laughs aloud at his simple joke quite unaware the rest of the family are just blandly staring at him.

Ma makes one of her rare comments. "Oh, our Jack, you'll learn one day, now eat up before your stew gets cold."

This is what I love about my family, for whatever troubles may befall us, we can always rely on one or other of the brothers to brighten our day.

Chapter 3
Summer

Carrie Gibbs stands outside her run-down cottage, leaning against the post that strings the washing line down to the sturdy branches of the ash tree. My ma treasures these little moments of solitude and we know to respect that privacy. With her arms crossed to support her ample bosom she breathes in the early morning fresh air, knowing it will be short lived as the sun warms the land. Some days have been unbearable this year with the heat, making any work far harder to tackle. Right now, she is watching the antics of the raucous crows as they wrestle for space high up in its branches. These brief moments remind her of her weariness and creeping age but also serve to fill her with a sense of peace away from the crowded atmosphere of her home. However much she loves her brood, she also craves for a little solitude, a short time to think about their futures and count her blessings they are all in good health. She pushes the stray, grey hairs from her face and sighs, then stirring herself, she waddles her way along the rough path of chipped brick and ashes that leads to the end of the vegetable patch alongside the shared privy. However hard she tries to keep the place clean and sweet smelling with herbs and lavender hung upon an old nail, there is a persistent unpleasant smell that lingers, enough to make her girls wait until they are really desperate to make the trip, and then only arm in arm with one of the sisters.

It seems her old man Jacob is immune as he prefers to use the privy as his hiding place and spends quite some time down there.

She's seen a big change in him over the twenty odd years they have been wed, that once confident upright fellow, strong of arm and never work shy, who is now prone to black moods that become exacerbated when work dries up. She can clearly recall how many times the lads have come in to tell her their dad is drowning his sorrows down at the local inn. So right now she is really grateful that he has steady work and a regular wage in these summer months.

Earlier in April, word was passed around the local villages that new owners were taking over at nearby Branswick Hall and able men and boys were wanted to clear part of the overgrown woodland within their grounds. Carrie guiltily remembers how she practically pushed her older sons Henry and Tom out of the cottage, sending them off in due haste with their father in the hopes they would be all taken on. Henry, having proved himself as being skilled with the band saw, was taken on by Lord Gressingham's steward. His father Jacob was reluctantly taken on as one of the team to load the wagons with felled wood. With Joe having secured work at the stables, it meant a steady income for the family. Tom had slunk back, feigning lack of interest, pretending it wasn't right for him, when all along Carrie could feel the pain of his rejection. From his difficult birth it was clear to see he would struggle to hold down any regular work. Carrie knew folk called him simple, but he was special to her, and had a gentle nature, one ideally suited to caring for the hens they kept out in the back yard beyond the privy.

With a sigh Carrie bends down and pulls one of the cabbages from the vegetable bed, flicks off the stray caterpillars and heads for the cottage. I had crept downstairs and peered around the door trying not to startle her.

"Morning, Ma."

With a little jerk of surprise, Ma beams at me. "Hello me duck! You're a good girl to come down and help me. I reckon it'll be another hot one today."

Carrie reaches out and takes my hand, giving it a reassuring squeeze of affection as we head into the kitchen. There is an uneasy silence between us, as if neither wishes to speak but Ma takes charge and wheels round to face me, insisting I sit down.

"Now just you listen, my gal. I know there's something troubling you. I can see it in your eyes but whatever it is, there's always an answer and a way to sort it out. Has that young Bertie been a-hassling you? He's a nice enough fellow, but still a bit silly when he fools around with that little bunch of pals he got to know from the town."

I try to remain calm although worrying thoughts are churning over in my mind, but with the mention of Bertie, I end up grinning at my mother.

"No Ma, he's just a bit of fun and likes to come round for one of his chats. I think he just wants me to agree with all his outrageous ideas so it makes him feel important! Everything's OK, Ma."

She seems to hesitate before firing her next salvo. "Now you haven't gone and done something bad up at that vicarage, have you gal?"

I can feel my face beginning to redden so I blurt out, "No Ma, I'm just lucky as I get to do my work and no one ever complains, so it's a lot easier than when I used to scrub for Old Mrs Barlow."

There is a sudden clattering as the family clamber around the breakfast table. I am spared from further conversation, suppressing the strong desire to tell my mother how different my role is now. Instead, I turn to stir the large pan of porridge that simmers over the wood fired range. I have learnt to keep my thoughts to myself. My siblings are prone to be noisy and often argumentative at mealtimes, but I tend to remain quiet for secretly I'm dreaming of being free from them all. Today my younger sister Mary is greedily spooning her breakfast with just her eyes flicking from one to another as the morning banter continues. As she finishes she looks at me, peering through unruly, mousy ringlets. "Will you do my plaits, our Flo? Ma was too busy in the kitchen when I got down."

I tweak her still-scarred nose in a friendly gesture and nod my assent. "Hand over the ribbons, then, and I'll do it now."

Mary rummages in the pocket of her apron and dangles a single brown ribbon. "I lost the other one, but don't tell Ma or she'll have another go at me, promise?"

We move over towards the dresser and I grab a hairbrush and try to tame the unruly locks, pulling them into a single plait.

"What are you like, our Mary! Just don't lose that one today or else! There aren't many more days 'til school finishes, so are you learning anything at all, or is this heat making everyone drowsy?"

Mary turns and gives me an intense look.

"Did you know that Queen Victoria is eighty?!"

She stresses the last word in disbelief and I have to agree it sounds a great age. "Perhaps if you get all the jobs done for you, and you sit on a throne ordering your servants about, well maybe you do live much longer. We shall never know, Mary."

Even as I say those words, I feel somewhat ashamed. Surely, I can't be the only one to daydream about how lovely it would be to live in grandeur.

"Miss Cross also told us that some man has been sending words through the air! May said he must have been shouting very loud but Miss Cross said it was something about a radio and he had a funny name, I think it was Macaroni? Did you know about that, Flo?"

"My, you are becoming a clever young lass to know all these things, but lots of things are changing as we get older, and just think, it'll be 1900 next year and maybe that will bring us all good luck! Now shoo, or we'll all be late!"

Chapter 4
Decisions

It is becoming the hardest thing I have ever had to do, or so it seemed last night as I lay awake, churning my thoughts over and over. I needed to clarify what exactly my role would now become and in truth, part of me so loved my work in the kitchen that I felt a reluctance to abandon that. What did I know about being a companion?

I'd only once seen how the elderly Miss Baines was pushed around in her rickety wooden wheelchair by a rather austere grey-haired lady, who had a habit of glaring at any passers-by. Ma told us Miss Baines was a lady of means. She lived in the next village down our road and could afford to have a companion. My big brother Joe, who works for the Gressinghams up at the stables of Branswick Hall, thinks being a lady of means clearly applies to the grim-faced companion whose face was the meanest he'd ever set eyes on. My brothers and their little witticisms do make us laugh at times, but there may be some truth in their comments and I decide that maybe this is not for me. I don't want to end up like that, so as I slip out of our shared bed, wincing at the chilly floor beneath my feet, I vow to speak plainly to the Reverend this very morning.

Lizzie and Harriet follow soon after me, dressing hastily and descending to our kitchen. Lizzie is two years younger than me although she is as tall as I am, so we are often mistaken for twins, except she is the only one in the family with jet black hair. Pa teases Ma and reckons she must have had a secret rendezvous with the sweep, resulting in Lizzie having a very different appearance to the rest of us. We happen to know that one of Pa's brothers also has dark black hair, so take no notice of his little jibes. He loves us all, when he's sober and, in his chatty mood, he'll stress time and time again his love for us all and links it to our strongest talents. For Lizzie it's her sweet singing voice that he compares to that of an angel. I'm forever told it's my winning smile that is my saving grace, although there are times when that becomes very hard to achieve.

"Time you was off, girls."

Carrie is labouring at the stone sink, energetically scrubbing a pile of work shirts. Peering over her shoulder she gives us all a quick smile before returning to her work and we leave, walking arm in arm away from our cottage.

"I wish we had the day to ourselves, Flo," says Lizzie. "I reckon it'll be a scorcher. Don't really fancy being stuck indoors slaving for old Grumps. Wouldn't it be great if you and me could just slip through the fields and dangle our feet in the cool river water?"

"Oh, our Lizzie, you are a daydreamer! Best not think about such things and do what we are tasked to do, and anyway, if it's hot this Sunday, we could still do it then."

I feel rather sorry for our kid sister. When she got the job in service for Mr Graves, the local town grocer, it appeared at first that she had landed a good position. It turns out that he is a miserable and hard taskmaster. That's why he's known as Grumpy Graves. She is charged with keeping the rooms above his shop in good order, but more recently he's made her stay on to do extra work. I've seen her come home with her fingers sore from rubbing his precious collection of spiked fireside brasses and he has also made her tackle some of the gardening work. Ma got quite angry when she saw the scratches on her daughter's arms. Mr Graves had insisted Lizzie stay and help clear some wild brambles in his overgrown garden backing into the house and shop. She had not dared to refuse for fear of losing her job, but it is hardly what is expected of a lowly domestic. He had thrust a slightly chipped glass jar of relish into her hands by way of recompense. Ma was furious at this payoff and would have thrown that jar out into the yard there and then, had not Henry, our eldest brother, grabbed her hand and made her see sense.

"No point in wasting it, Ma. It'll go down fine with a good slice of ham."

Thus, the relish was placed upon the shelf for future use and Ma had turned away, muttering under her breath.

We reach the crossroads, hug and go our separate ways, still a little bleary eyed in the early morning heat haze. My heart is heavy for her ordeal as I know she is not happy right now. Sometimes I wish I could get Lizzie some work up at the vicarage with me. I have even contemplated asking the Reverend if he could create a post for her, but now realise that is completely out of the question. My path takes me along a pleasant country lane and my spirits are lifted by the birdsong from the hedgerows. I go over and over in my head the words I need to say. I have finally made up my mind and must really inform the Reverend as sensitively as I can, so as not to offend, but I really feel my place is as a cook, not a companion.

A little knot of apprehension tightens in my stomach as I near the vicarage. An imposing stone building, it stands overlooking the triangular village green adjacent to the parish church. I step around the side of the house to access the back door, knowing I must choose the right moment to speak with the Reverend. Now, after grabbing my work apron, all my focus is upon my daily work, or so I anticipate, for at that moment Miss Ophelia bounces into the kitchen, eyes glistening and eager to chat.

"Isn't it wonderful? Papa has spoken to you and now you're to be my best friend! You shall always be known as Florence, for I'm sure that is your proper Christian name and it sounds much grander. Come with me! I've made plans for us today and it means you can leave all this to the Millie for once!"

With that, and before I can catch my breath to answer, she grabs my left hand and leads me into the drawing room. The contrast between our clothes becomes suddenly apparent. Ophelia is wearing a pretty, pale blue dress, rather full in the skirt, and her auburn hair hangs loose in a mass of ringlets. I am feeling shamed by my coarse brown skirt, but am just grateful I had chosen a clean white blouse to go with it.

"Papa says there is no work today and so…"

"But the lunch," I interject. "They're my duties, Miss Ophelia. I need to make a start for the Reverend."

She firmly stamps her feet impetuously and shakes her curls. "No! No! No! Father has engaged a cook to cover for the day and Millie will be helping her. We are going out for a treat! Now, come with me."

This isn't meant to happen and I feel speechless and powerless to react, so I meekly follow her upstairs to her private bedroom.

All my good intentions have evaporated and it seems pointless trying to argue with her insistence. I find myself in a whirl of colourful dresses that Ophelia draws forth from her closet, as she chooses a delicate lemon design patterned with miniature buds and roses.

"There. That's perfect for you, as it is going to be a warm day! Let's find you some lighter shoes for you to wear and be comfortable."

She rummages in a series of boxes and shows me the most beautiful little silken shoes. My heart skips a beat as I survey them. However, try as I might, with the size of my feet being significantly larger than hers, I sadly have to admit defeat, hoping the length of this pretty dress will disguise my plain working shoes. She turns me to face a long, freestanding mirror and I gasp as I see my reflection. I'm in a fairytale world; I am like Cinderella transformed and I like what I see. If this is a foretaste of my future, then I will grab it with both hands and embrace the experience.

"I think you might just need a little shawl, just in case."

With that she drapes one around my shoulders. I feel quite overcome by her fastidious attention.

18

"Miss Ophelia, this is most kind of you…" I don't manage to finish my sentence because she is still fussing over me, adding a matching white ribbon to my tied back brown hair.

"Please, please, I insist that you stop this *Miss* nonsense when we are together. I want us to be the best of friends and today is a new beginning for us both. From now you must call me Ophelia – no arguing! – but when we go out together, we shall be the Misses Florence and Ophelia! I think we are now ready for the little surprise!"

Chapter 5
Transformation

If I live to be a hundred I don't think I'll ever forget that enchanting day when I was transformed into Miss Florence, companion and friend to Miss Ophelia. It was so magical; I felt as if I were in a dream as I was helped into the horse-drawn gig by Reverend Henderson himself. He must have hired it, along with a driver, just for this special occasion. Sitting alongside his excited daughter, we three jolted along, sometimes hanging on to the side rails as the gig veered around the bends in the country lanes. A large food hamper had been wedged somewhat uncomfortably between our legs, but it all added to the novelty of the day. The Reverend seemed as excited as his daughter, his little dark eyes twinkling, almost relishing the fact that I had absolutely no idea where we were heading for.

Once he caught me unawares by leaning forward and actually patting my knee, saying, "I'm sure you'll love it, Florence!"

I gave a hesitant smile that I hope disguised my still-confused feelings. Was I still in service or had all that been left behind? They were treating me like a member of the family and I was finding it hard to adapt to this freedom. I began to wonder if my fairytale would end in the same way and it would all be snatched away from me at sunset.

Our destination turned out to be a total surprise. The sturdy gig turned on to a long gravel drive bordered by giant copper beech trees; there ahead of us I could see a beautiful, shimmering lake rippling in the late morning sunlight and the sight was enchanting. All this beauty and I was unaware it existed and yet it was only a short distance from our little village. As we drew to a halt the driver jumped down and proffered his arm to steady us all as we stepped from our seats. The Reverend acknowledged this act with some coins and after speaking to the driver with further instructions, he lifted the picnic hamper, smiled broadly at us, then led the way down the grassy bank towards the water's edge.

"Isn't this just heaven, Florence? I do love coming here each year and I shall introduce you to our friends and we'll have a splendid time!"

Ophelia stands waving to a family who have their rugs laid upon the grass beneath the shade of a wafting willow tree. A stout gentleman, whose waistcoat refuses to stay completely buttoned, immediately stands to greet us with the broadest of smiles.

"Cedric Henderson! My dear fellow, and your lovely Ophelia. What a pleasure to greet you both and your pretty guest at this annual event! And by Jove, we seem to have luck on our side with the glorious weather. Ideal for the afternoon entertainment! Now, will you introduce me to this young lady?"

The Reverend extends a hand and cordially greets this gentleman, stopping to also acknowledge his seated wife and family before turning to face me.

"Today we have the pleasure of joining Mr and Mrs Wagstaff with their young son Gerald and the delightful Miss Clara. Now let me introduce you to my daughter's friend, Florence. This is her first time at the Gressingham Gathering, so I'm sure you'll make her very welcome."

I know my winning smiles will help break the ice and I'm so relieved that his introduction was brief and hopefully will not lead to many questions, for I'm sure I'll be completely tongue tied. With our rugs spread, Ophelia and I kneel down. I sit sideways making sure my shoes are well hidden beneath the swirl of my beautiful dress. I vow to only speak when spoken to, and spend the next few minutes eyeing the seated figures.

The Reverend is eager to give me an explanation about the gathering. "You see, Florence, we have brought you here because each year special invitations are sent out to the gentry in the county and these private grounds are part of the estate. Lord and Lady Gressingham open it for this special day of festivities. Look, you can see all the people who have come and there will be many more converging in their carriages. Later on we shall venture on to the lake itself!"

My heart momentarily skips a beat, as I have a fear of deep water. Family legends tells of a past ancestor who was drowned at sea from a sailing ship and lost to the oceans, and that very thought has since scared me whenever I am near a swollen stream after heavy rainfall. Now I'm just absorbing the fact that I am sitting here, in the grounds of a grand estate, wearing this delicate dress, and it feels very most pleasant.

Ophelia claps her hands in excitement and leans towards me. "Now, I want to introduce my friend Clara. Oh, do come and sit with us. We haven't met since last year's festivities."

Ophelia pats the rug and we shuffle up to make room for Clara. I regard her rather slim frame and pallid disposition and wonder what ails her. Ophelia is keen to fill me in on how they first met.

"Naturally, Papa has known Clara's family a while, but we met here last year for the first time and then discovered we both share the same school tutor!"

The girls titter at some private little joke as Ophelia continues.

"It's just that he fidgets the whole of the time and has this terrible habit of..." After a calculated pause she continues, "Sniffing and loudly sneezing!"

At this, Clara clasps her tiny hand to her mouth, suppressing another laugh. They paint an image of an insecure young man who is trying to earn his living at the homes of the wealthy, whilst possibly suffering from the summer fevers that affect some country dwellers. My brother Joe has those very symptoms and we call it hay fever, when the grasses are well

22

grown and the pollen spreads freely in the surrounding air. I simply have no knowledge about private tutors, having had a simple education in our local board school in the nearby town of Felborough. Thankfully, the young lad Gerald diverts everyone's attention by standing abruptly, pointing over the water and shouting aloud: "Papa! Papa! The boats are being untied!"

All eyes swivel towards along the jetty where several rowing boats had been safely moored. Young men are loosening the ropes, as a small party stand waiting to get on. I've seen boats similar to this on our local river during the duck hunting season. One of the boats is pushed off and I can hear the jolly laughter from the party of four on board as they swing out unsteadily and one man rows clumsily across the lake.

After that, Mrs Wagstaff has gone into an organising mode as picnics were unpacked and generously shared between the two families. To this day I have absolutely no idea who had prepared the food we had brought along. I politely answered questions without giving too much away and, after a while, began to enjoy this new friendship with a feeling I was fitting in well. Later, it was the Reverend who insisted we too go out in one of the rowing boats, reassuring my worried face that it was perfectly safe as he would be in charge of the oars. To my absolute amazement I found it a charming experience, listening to the swish of the strokes, hearing the ducks quack, then scrabble away from our advancing craft as it was steadily rowed around the lake. I even dared to trail my hand in the cool water and boldly gazed at my reflection in complete awe of my being there. At one point, Ophelia suggested we both look up at the changing cloud patterns that floated across the clear blue sky.

It was beginning to feel so perfect until we returned and neared the jetty, when to my horror I identified my young brother Jack, who had plainly been hired to steady and secure the boats before and after use. As he looked up and recognised me, our eyes locked with stunned disbelief and I felt powerless to acknowledge him. Ophelia was giggling as she stood up first, somewhat unsteady with the rocking motion. Jack courteously offered a steadying arm to support her, but all the time his eyes were fast set on mine. No words were exchanged between us and his look turned to one of contempt as he roughly hauled me out of the boat and on to the jetty. Finally, the Reverend leapt out in an exuberant manner after his rowing adventures. All smiles, he placed his embracing arms around my shoulders and swept me along, with his daughter on the other side. As we headed back to our picnic site, I glanced back over my shoulder, only to register the cold expression on my brother's face. That was the moment my euphoria seemed to melt away and I realised it was going to be even harder to explain my situation to my family.

Chapter 6
Envy

There is little time for Jack to dwell on the shock of seeing his sister Flo as the ever-increasing queue of eager boaters line up patiently along the wooden jetty. His focus is on preparing the next empty craft, holding fast to the mooring ropes and proffering his arm to steady the giddy ladies in their full skirts, several fearful of tumbling into the boat, but who are eager to be out on the lake. He stands a little in awe of the upstart young gentlemen who completely ignore him, too full of their own importance and out to impress their excitable companions. As one fellow grabs the oars, Jack pushes the boat away with a disdainful shove of his foot, then turns swiftly to accept the rope from an incoming craft about to moor. He puts all previous thoughts to the back of his mind for he knows this offer of work for the day will bring a decent reward. With an eager stream of visitors during the heat of the afternoon, Jack is sometimes tipped by well-dressed gents with a few coins which greatly pleases him. Tucked well down into his trouser pockets, he feels pleased with himself although his clothes seem far too restricting for such a warm day. Ma had insisted he wear a high neck shirt with the jacket he had for church. It is becoming more uncomfortable as the hours passed and he has to pull the neck away to waft some cooler air onto his face.

As the afternoon passes and the queue dwindles, Jack stands back against a sturdy post on the jetty and takes a moment to survey the scene. He can see family groups on the opposite side of the shimmering lake. There is an impromptu cricket match taking place over to the right, from which he can hear loud whoops and cries as lads are bowled out. Right now, he is scanning the grassy banks trying to identify the tall black coated gentleman who had been paying so much attention to his sister. It seems an impossible task beside which, several parties have congregated further down near some tents so he is unable to find them however hard he looks around. The last two little rowing boats are slowly edging towards the bank and Jack feels a buoyancy, knowing his work will soon be finished and he can then head for home and peel off his warm jacket for some relief from the day's heat.

Walking home beneath the shade of the overhanging tree branches, Jack feels free and slightly euphoric. He keeps a firm hand in his pocket, tapping the generous payment he has received, his jacket thrown over one shoulder and his shirt unbuttoned. His thoughts are still on the day's shock events, but now there are niggling doubts. Perhaps in the heat of the day he had mistaken someone else for his sister; he'd once heard his father say that everyone in the world has a double somewhere and anyway it couldn't have been her for he knew she had work up at the vicarage. At that he completely dismisses the foolish notion and sets to, whistling a merry tune as he wends his way back through the lanes towards Higher Weldon and conscious of his empty stomach that anticipates a welcome meal when he returns home. Mary is eager to know how it all went.

"Here's our Jack! How was it today? Were there hundreds of people there? Do tell!"

Mary rushes to greet him, jumping up and down, her eyes glistening with anticipation of hearing about her brother's day.

"Leave the lad alone, our Mary! Let him be 'til he's had summat to eat."

Ma has ladled a helping of warm food onto his plate.

"Eat up lad, your dad got lucky today and bagged a rabbit, no questions asked!"

The stew is good and Jack makes short work of eating it, expressing his gratitude with a generous belch of approval. Lizzie, who is sitting sewing by the nearest window can't help but smile at the way Jack is trying to imitate his father's ways, and only because he is absent from the kitchen. Ma gives him a stern disapproving look but feels so grateful for the extra money he handed her on his return, she hasn't the heart to chastise him.

"Gosh Ma, you should have seen the toffs in their fancy gear arriving in all manner of carriages and carts. Great big flowery hats and men in bright waistcoats, and carrying rugs or seats and baskets of food and drink, kids playing bat and ball, some flying kites, one group got together for a cricket match, and nearly all of 'em wanting to get out on the little rowing boats. That kept me busy all afternoon, but it wasn't too hard. Pity they only do it once a year or I'd be a rich man!"

His brother Henry has been listening at the end of the table, he too has been enjoying his hot meal, and now he stands and approaches Jack, laying his worn scarred hands upon the lad's shoulders.

"Just think on young Jackie, you might have had a good day today, with folk in a jovial mood, but if you gets a job up on that there estate for good, you'll be under their thumbs and might regret it. Now why don't you follow me and feel the freedom of doing good honest work amongst the trees where no one bothers you?"

Henry cuffs him affectionately across his tousled brown hair and heads for the back door just as I return home. He grins as he passes me, adjusting his cap in its usual jaunty angle.

Carrie is first to comment. "They kept you a bit late today Flo, didn't they? Will you wanting me to do a dish for you?"

I shake my head whilst lowering my small basket alongside the back door.

"No thanks Ma, I've already eaten today."

With a big smile I kiss my mother upon the left cheek, then that smile evaporates as my eyes lock on those of my brother Jack. My heart is pounding with the fear of what he'll say, but no words come, and he sits, giving only a silent, accusatory glare before he pushes back his chair and walks out of the kitchen and heads for the garden. Carrie is blissfully unaware of this situation, clearing plates to the sink whilst I am desperate to confide in her and seek some honest advice, hoping that she can find a moment when we can talk in private, away from the family but there are more important things to do first. I need to face my brother and speak clearly to him.

"Did you want anything picking from the garden tonight, Ma? I reckon from those dark clouds we're in for some heavy showers soon, might be safest to get the veggies in for tomorrow?"

Carrie pauses at the table, stands to think a while and nods.

"Some of them carrots and a good-sized onion would be good, our Flo! But don't you go getting your nice work clothes dirty from the garden mud!"

There's a certain irony in those innocent words as I think once more about the beautiful lemon dress I had been wearing earlier that afternoon. Miss Ophelia had insisted I was to keep it, but this posed all manner of problems and feigning a headache after being in the sun that afternoon, I had fled to the safety of the vicarage kitchen where behind a locked door I could swiftly change back into my normal clothes. Nothing had quite worked out as I had planned, for my good intentions to refuse the offer of being her companion had simply evaporated as we enjoyed each other's company. Now I am burdened with guilt as I recall the joy at my brief transformation into the world of the gentry.

Ducking beneath the drooping bough of a plum tree, I approach the vegetable patch and spot Jack sitting on the upturned wheelbarrow whittling a piece of softwood, biting his lip as he concentrates.

"Jack, it's not what you think."

I realise that just saying this might sound rather feeble and unbelievable.

"I was just there, for one day, to keep Miss Henderson company as she so insisted. It was all a bit stupid, I know. I'm not even sure why I agreed to do it."

Jack stares coldly at me and fires the next comment.

"Well it looked like you was enjoying every bit of it, Miss Lah-di-da! And you never even spoke to me!"

He throws the half-shaped piece of wood to the ground in a fit of disgust.

"Go and live with them, see if I care!"

As he bends to retrieve his bit of wood, he lowers his eyes yet I can see the tears that have welled up, tears of frustration tinged with a certain envy of what he had witnessed that day, of how things could be, if only you were well placed in life.

Chapter 7
Resolve

That night I make up my mind and vow to speak with Reverend Henderson at the first opportunity tomorrow morning, but I am thankful my sisters are distracting me right now with their incessant chatter of something and nothing as they usually do, to put the world to rights. We are used to sharing a bed, and Harriet is in one of her gossipy moods, swooning over one of the lads who works in the shoe factory.

"Oh, he's got these lovely brown eyes and he's tall and handsome, and he says he'll escort me up to the Meadow Field when the fairground arrives next week! He's seen posters in the Felborough shops, that's how he knows."

"He might just be telling you that so as to get you up there and do naughty things to you!"

Lizzie nudges Harriet as she teases her and they both laugh quietly beneath the quilt. This is what I love about my family, and even though we each dream of having a bed to our self, this intimacy is all we have ever known and I find it heart-warming.

"Maybe he already has!"

Lizzie and I are momentarily stunned, but then she has a habit of always trying to shock us with her outrageous comments.

"Harriet! He never has?"

She does not answer, but instead turns over on to her front and pulls most of the bedding off Lizzie and myself. But two against one, and a hefty tug in the opposite direction and we are able to settle down for the night.

I have a rather battered black umbrella that was loaned to me from the vicarage and it is much appreciated this morning, as the rain falls lightly but persistently on my short walk to work. I am feeling far more confident and am going over in my mind the words I shall say to define my position. The house sounds very still and quiet, although when I peer through into the hallway I detect a scratching noise and realise the Reverend is busy writing. There is no sign or sound from Miss Ophelia, for which I am very grateful. I am content to be back in my kitchen doing what I love best. When I eventually hear him stirring and walking about, I head towards his study and knock firmly upon the door. I am expecting to hear a resonant "Come!", but instead am confronted by the bearded face of the Reverend as he opens the door.

"Florence! I had hoped to have a further chat with you today to thank you for accompanying us yesterday, and now this seems an opportune time, but firstly do come in and take a seat."

My heart is racing, but I am resolved to say my piece.

"Please, sir, I was flattered to be asked to join you and Miss Ophelia and can't thank you enough for your kindness to me, but I need my job here as your cook far more and I don't want to appear rude, sir, but I don't think being a companion is for me."

There. I've said it, and all that I can see as I watch the Reverend's face are his understanding eyes as he nods in a thoughtful way.

"My dear girl, I can see you've had a lot to think about. I certainly don't want to replace you as our cook. You've been a blessing for us. I think we shall be ever grateful to your dear mother for how she taught you. And Florence – I shall still call you Florence – your delicious pastry would please the Lord himself! Let me make myself clear. There are some occasions when I'd like you to accompany my daughter, just as a friend, for being an only child she can get rather lonely. She has persistently been begging me to persuade you, and I trust yesterday proved a pleasant time for you both."

I am taken aback by this speech, but am proud I spoke out and relieved that my position has been clarified.

"Thank you, sir, for your understanding. I very much enjoyed being invited to go with you and your daughter, especially being on the water. So, I am happy to help in that way and very grateful to you for keeping me on."

I am beginning to feel somewhat flustered by this turn of events, but mightily relieved I can spare my family any disgrace.

"I best be getting back, sir, to my duties. Thank you again."

As I stand up ready to leave, the Reverend kindly moves to open the door for me and I feel humbled at his kindness.

"Oh, and let me add I am more than happy for you to use our little library should you wish to read any of the books. Ophelia will be down later to talk with you and possibly arrange when it will be convenient for you to accompany her on another outing. Thank you, Florence, and we'll see you at lunchtime."

I can't believe my good fortune and inevitably I break into a broad smile of appreciation at his kindness as I leave the study. The relief I feel having tackled this sticky issue is very satisfying and I feel almost lightheaded as I enter the kitchen and throw myself into creating a special lunch for them both. Today I have some fish prepared steeped in a rich wine sauce and I feel quite pleased with the fancy moulded milk jelly that I plan to serve with little madeleine fingers.

Chapter 8
The Viewing

I've known Albert from my childhood as we were more or less brought up together. We live in the end part of the cottage, it having been divided with separate doors for three families. The Mason family have some rooms in the central part, including Albert and his four siblings, and then there's just the widowed John Groom in a single room that used to part of the cow shed at the far end.

Albert is always around, in and out of our kitchen, pestering Ma for a spare apple or sliver of her lardy cake we know she keeps hidden in a battered tin beneath the kitchen sink. When we were young we'd play out on the flagstones outside our back doors, spending hours flipping flints of slate to see who could reach the edge of the path first, or having conker fights each autumn. He's fun to be with and can be quite witty at times, although Pa thinks he's a cocky young devil. My older sister Sue seems intent on us making a go of it, but I don't think that he'd be the right fellow for me. After all, he's got bright ginger hair; I know that means they have fiery tempers and I wouldn't want that in a husband! He's just good fun to be with, although I do wish he wouldn't hang around on the chance of chatting to me.

He also spends time gazing at my body and I'm slightly fearful of those earnest looks, for it sometimes makes me feel very self-conscious of my growing bosoms. There's always a good reason for me to excuse myself on the grounds I have to go in and help Ma prepare our meals and it's done with a certain amount of relief. Unlike my sisters Sue and Harriet, who are intent on bagging the first man that pays them attention, I am currently beginning to enjoy a little taste of singular freedom up at the vicarage.

Ever since July, the doubts I experienced have been eased as I adapt to my dual role, although I never fully explain my elevated position to my sisters.

I have hinted to my mother about a couple of outings and she just listens and makes no comment. As far as they are concerned, I'm still just the daily cook, perhaps just mentioning now and then that I have assisted the young lady with a few minor tasks, like helping her choose what to wear for a special occasion. I never tell of the times I, too, am privileged to wear delightful dresses that seem to be solely for me now, or of the places we visit.

Only last week I'd been summoned with a request to accompany Miss Ophelia to a private viewing of watercolour paintings to be held in one of the wings of Branswick Hall. She had been most enthusiastic and insisted on attending.

"Florence, we simply must go for I've heard such fine things about Mr Henry Stannard. I've been told he paints delightful little scenes of our whole district."

Not wanting to appear foolish, I had wholeheartedly agreed, but had no idea who this gentleman was. I felt rather grateful when she explained further.

"It's all rather exciting because Father has met him once. He's quite a celebrity and was born in our own county of Bedfordshire! The invitation is for next Tuesday morning, Florence, and you won't be asked to do a lunch as Father will be visiting a nearby parish. We'll be hiring the gig, so I am hoping we don't get a sudden September shower of rain or we shall end up looking like water paintings ourselves!"

I have to smile at her exuberance, for with any event away from the confines of her home I begin to share her excitement at thoughts of another expedition to broaden my horizons.

So here I am, sitting alongside Ophelia as we jolt down that familiar gravel drive, admiring the golden beauty of the beech leaves overhead and relieved the day has stayed dry, although there are several menacing clouds that threaten to mar the occasion for us later. Today I am wearing a long, dark, navy skirt with a matching jacket more suited to the cooler air. I now have a special closet at the vicarage where these outfits are kept for me. I happen to know they once belonged to Ophelia, but am told to treat them as my own. It still seems surreal with this subterfuge, but when these special days occur I feel like a totally different person, and I like that feeling.

Whereas on the previous occasion we had taken a right turn towards the lake on that symbolic July day, today our driver veers left and then the full glory of Branswick Hall appears before me. I feel great awe at its size as I gaze at the long, wide frontage with its elaborate carving above that seems to resemble the Christmas garlands we weave out of ivy and fern to decorate our cottage rooms. I try to imagine Lord and Lady Gressingham living in such grand style as I look up at the many windows there. To either side there are imposing rectangular wings that jut out, and it is towards one of these that our driver heads.

"Oh, Florence, isn't this going to be grand? I wonder how many other guests have been invited and whether or not the famous man himself will be there."

I step down after Ophelia and she insists on firmly holding my hand, although I suspect that is more of a reassurance and that underneath her bubbly exterior she is feeling as nervous as I am.

A smartly dressed footman is standing to attention outside, clad in his dark russet brown livery. He surveys the invitation card that Ophelia holds, then ushers us through the open glass doors into an imposing corridor with white marble statues on each side. For one brief moment I feel out of my depth again, but she is still gripping tight to my hand and that feels very comforting as we enter the large room where several large wooden stands are supporting the paintings.

There are about a dozen people in the room, many up close to view the scenes and some light-hearted laughter from a couple sitting on the window seat.

A kind-hearted gentleman approaches us and introduces himself.

"Ladies, you are both very welcome. My name is Sir Edward Grant and I am sponsoring this private viewing of Henry Stannard, our talented local artist. If you'd allow me, I would be honoured to escort you around these delightful works of art so that you may absorb their beauty. Now, to whom do I have the pleasure of talking?"

Ophelia is accustomed to such civility and speaks out clearly.

"How very kind of you, Sir Edward. This is Miss Florence Gibbs, a dear friend, and I am Miss Ophelia Henderson. We are so looking forward to seeing everything."

I dip my head and smile, for that act bolsters my confidence to face further questioning. I am spared that as we follow his guiding hands towards the first of the delicate drawings in pastel colours. I've never before seen an actual painting and am quite bowled over by the familiar scenes of rural life that are portrayed, although in my experience they look too good to be true.

I whisper to Ophelia, "They're very grand, although I doubt if the roads are ever as clean as he has painted them. There's no sign of all the mud!"

"My dear Florence, no one would buy a painting of a muddy place! It's so much nicer to have a pretty scene upon a wall to satisfy your soul. Look at this one! How charming with all the pale lilacs trees surrounding this dear little thatched cottage! I think I shall be inspired to find my own palette of watercolours. I seem to recall Mama gave me a set when I was much younger, but I wasn't very keen to try at the time. This will be our new project, Florence. You and I shall learn to paint together!"

Her enthusiasm for new ventures amuses me and I have to agree with her.

"Then we shall become the new artists and have our famous pieces on show just like this famous artist today!"

I feel very brave coming out with this bold statement and we both laugh at the ludicrous suggestion and move on. Sir Edward excuses himself to greet other newcomers and we are at liberty to see the paintings and even take a refreshing drink from a servant holding a large silver tray of glasses. I had assumed it to be a refreshing type of lemonade, so am rather startled to feel the fizzing bubbles in my mouth. It's the turn of Ophelia to whisper in my ear.

"This is champagne. Papa says I'm still too young to be tasting it, so we must keep this little secret to ourselves, Florence!"

I swiftly decide this is not the drink for me after a mere sip or two, and return my half-full glass. It is simply taken back by the expressionless tray holder. However, Ophelia seems happy to slowly sip her drink as we circulate around the remainder of the art work. I wonder if the objective of this viewing is for anyone to actually buy a watercolour, and am left imagining the sort of prices they would have to pay. Back at home we have only one faded print on the parlour wall of Queen Victoria as a young girl; we'd been told Great-Grandad had bought it off a market stall. I vow then and there that when I am a wealthy woman, I too will be able to buy a genuine painting. Perhaps I'm beginning to believe that possibility actually exists for me.

Chapter 9
September

My life is more settled now, and because I've been training Millie to assist with preparing and serving meals, I no longer feel guilty about leaving her to cope in the kitchen whilst I am called to be with Ophelia. These are days I really treasure. Of late, we both have been attempting to grasp the fine art of watercolour painting as she had so desired. There is a wooden gazebo in one corner of the garden and that is where we set up strange wooden stands that I've learnt to call easels. From our covered position we have a pleasant view of all aspects of the garden in the afternoon light, so our little sketches can be of the colourful birds that drop on to the lawn, the delicate blossoms that fill the air with their sweet scent, or of the textured stone wall with its variety of climbing plants. As autumn comes ever closer, the leaves are dropping fast from the azaleas, so today I have suggested we try and paint the colourful patterns they are making on the ground.

"I think this is rather a good idea, Florence. Don't you just love the vibrant red and orange? I can't quite get the exact colour match; perhaps a shade more vermillion? There!"

I look over at her intricate design and know instinctively it is far better than my humble attempt.

"Oh Miss Ophelia, it looks good enough to be chosen as a wonderful pattern for a floral dress. Perhaps you should consider going to art school, for you certainly have a talent for designing."

She shakes her head then gazes up into the sky.

"Papa has his plans for me and it means I shall be needed to help him in his parish work. Sadly, there are no funds to let me indulge that way. Oh no! I do believe I felt rain just then, and can you see that dark cloud overhead? Come on Florence, time to get back!"

I can't believe how quickly the rain begins to fall in earnest as we scrabble to rescue our little paintings, water jars and brushes, before running as fast as we can to the safety of the house. Even that short distance means we both have a soaking and we stand under the safety of the back porch, laughing at our bedraggled appearance.

Up in Ophelia's bedroom I towel her wet hair and she insists on doing the same for me. These are the special moments I feel part of her family to the point of forgetting my own. Then I'm reminded of my promise that I have agreed to go with my sisters to the fair at the weekend. I wonder if she is ever allowed to attend.

"Ophelia, do you ever go to see the fair when it comes to town? We love it when they set up in Meadow Field each year. My sisters get so excited to see the bright lights everywhere, especially on the Gallopers! It's always a thrill to take a ride and feel the air rushing past you as it spins faster and faster!"

She studies my eager face with a quizzical look, stretching out her hands to touch mine.

"Father is not very fond of such attractions and although I've seen them setting up in the field in past years, he warns me of the undesirables that go there and says I would not be safe with pickpockets who prey on others. Oh Florence, would it be wise for you to go? I'd simply hate it if you were to fall victim to one of those rogues."

Now I'm at a loss to know how to respond to her plea. This annual event is often a highlight for many families, brightening the darker evenings, adding excitement with its spectacular rides and sideshows. I feel a certain sadness that Ophelia has been denied these pleasures, but accept her reasoning.

"I might go or I might not. It will all depend on the weather, for if this rain continues the ground gets very churned up and spoils your boots."

As soon as I've uttered these words I feel ashamed. Oh why, oh why didn't I say shoes? It serves to remind me of my roots and I feel a fraud for covering up my true intention. I stand and politely say

"Thank you for today, Ophelia. I've had a very pleasant afternoon, but will leave you now if that's all right."

"I've loved having your company, Florence; it makes me so happy these days!"

I check in at the kitchen and find that Millie has coped well in my absence and has laid out a platter of cold chicken to serve later, so I am free to leave and head for home. She gives me a look of mild curiosity, but dares not to question my absences or the freedom I seem to been given. It has been such a happy day for me knowing I am needed by someone, and I stroll home humming a little tune, feeling very lucky. I've taken to imagining what life could be like if I were to be whisked away, dreaming of the special days when I can wear those becoming dresses that Ophelia has donated to me, imagining what it must be like to be waited on.

I'm so busy with all these impulsive thoughts that I suddenly jerk as a bicycle swerves just ahead of me and I'm brought down to earth by the grinning red face of young Albert.

"Haven't seen you around much lately, Flo. Mind if I walk with you?"

He leaps athletically from the saddle and proceeds to walk by my side, pushing the bike expertly with just his right hand.

"Well, Albert, I don't seem to have seen you around either."

I turn to look at him and am a little surprised to see how tall he has become, and when he gazes back at me I'm shocked to find my heart skips a beat.

With a slight stutter, his words come tumbling out. "I-I was wondering if you'd come to the fair with me on Saturday? Well, I mean you and your sisters, of course, so we could all stick together. What do you say, Flo?"

This is all rather unexpected, but pleasing nevertheless, and with a wry smile I accept his offer. "Do you think you can cope with four of us, Albert? We all want to go."

Rounding the last bend, we approach the cottages that we share. I want him to know I am grateful for asking if he could accompany us, for strangely Ophelia's words of warning are still fresh in my ears.

"Ma will feel a lot happier knowing we will be chaperoned. We are planning to leave late afternoon, to be there for when the bright lights are switched on. Thanks, Bertie. Thanks."

I quite shock myself that I have just called him Bertie out loud, but his presence has left me with a warm feeling and I can't wait for Saturday to come.

Chapter 10
The Fair

Much to my dismay, I wake on the day of the fair to the persistent sound of rain, which dampens my anticipation. Harriet has been extremely restless, tossing through the night and briefly waking me. Once or twice, I thought I heard her sniffing and muttering, although that could have been in her sleep. She rises early, stepping clumsily over me, then merely wipes her face with the wash rag, before fumbling into her clothes. Her actions stir the rest of us.

"Oh Harriet, why did you have to wake me? I was having such a dreamy dream of sitting at a table with loads of spicy, rich cakes, and I was just going to reach for one when you woke me! I hate you, Harriet!"

Mary sits in her corner bunk and pouts, but it is short lived. "It's today, isn't it? Yes, yes, and we're going to the fair!"

Now she is up, clapping her hands and jumping for joy at the prospect.

I am content to stretch into the warm space Harriet has just vacated for a few moments more.

"Not until later, you crazy goose, and maybe by then the rain will have stopped. Ma will expect us to go into town as usual and then Albert is kindly calling to escort us up to the fields."

"Ooh! Albert fancies you!"

"Don't be silly, our Mary. He's just being thoughtful."

Harriet has hurriedly dressed and sweeps past us with a blank look upon her face.

"I shan't be coming with you, so don't wait for me to get back from work."

The abruptness of her words startles both myself and Lizzie, who is now hunched up in our bed, rubbing the dust from her eyes.

"Someone got out of the wrong side of the bed, didn't they!"

With our bed wedged against the inner wall, it's pretty obvious there is only one way to get out! Something about Harriet's behaviour unsettles me, but I soon dismiss those ideas and rise to face the new day. I think nothing more about her as we shall be busy doing our messages. I am spared my work as Ophelia is out with her father visiting relatives, but Ma likes one or other of us to pick up some provisions from the market stalls in the local town of Felborough.

By mid-afternoon the rain has stopped, and puddles can be seen in the ruts of the road. It makes me somewhat hesitant about venturing out to the fair, as I know too well that the fields will be churned up with mud and we shall have to keep to the drier patches of ground as we go round the amusements and sideshows.

Lizzie is watching out of the front parlour window for Albert to arrive. She is warmly wrapped up and raring to go.

"What time did he say, Flo? I can't see him yet."

She looks left and right, silently wishing for him to appear, but knowing Albert, he's more likely to come directly to our back door. After all, it is the only door to our little section of cottage.

"He said after four, because by the time we've walked up there it'll be getting dark and the bright lights will be on by then. Mary, you'd better put your cloak on now so we are all ready."

"Do you think the Gallopers will be there this time? I shall try and get on the biggest one there and that's the golden hen "cos I think he's the best!"

Ma is sitting quietly to one corner of the parlour where we are waiting. She is engrossed with her lace making, swiftly challenging the bobbins at such a rate you can barely see them

43

for speed. But then she has to work quickly, for even the long strips of fine lace that she produces are sold on to dealers for meagre amounts of money. She looks up at us three girls, as we stand fidgeting in anticipation, waiting for our escort. In her soft voice she reminisces: "I used to love it when the fair came round. Of course, that was in the village where I was born. It was only a small one then, none of these new-fangled machines. I remember the old chap Nobby, who'd stand there for hours winding this huge handle to turn the swinging chairs, in the rain or in the fine, and oh we did have fun. Now, look sharp, lasses; that's Albert knocking now, so off you go and enjoy yourselves, and stick with him all the time!"

I feel quite heady about our little jaunt through the village and out towards Meadow Field, and Albert keeps us amused with his little comments.

"Do you realise if that roundabout goes anticlockwise, you only get six turns, 'cos it's slowing down, see?"

Mary is listening intently, her mind whirring, but not putting her off her big intention of grabbing the golden cockerel. Albert can see her dilemma and grins.

"Ah, but if they wind it up clockwise, then it'll go much faster and I reckon you'll get almost a dozen times round!"

Lizzie and I laugh at the nonsense of it all, although Mary has been convinced.

"I shall definitely wait for it to go the right way round then!"

With a curt nod of her head, she has made up her own mind. "You are a tease, Bertie."

I find myself whispering to him as he strolls beside me. I have to acknowledge he's fun to be with, and I feel safe when he's around, more so as we make our tracks through an open gate towards the vibrant lights of the fairground.

Lizzie and I stand to the side of a coconut shy, absorbing the smells and sounds that seem to emanate from every direction. With the raucous showmen bawling their wares, blinking lights and the constant throb of the shiny brass steam engines pulsing as they noisily drive the rides, we hardly know where to start. So, it is Mary, in her enthusiasm that drags us towards the grand galloping roundabout. It is gradually slowing down and she is so determined to get to that large cockerel, her pennies clutched tight in her hand. I watch as she jumps on with it still moving and before its occupants have dismounted.

"Oh, be careful, Mary!"

Albert darts forward, looking concerned and circling alongside the turning ride. He watches until with some relief, Mary manages to get her special one. The three of us clap with satisfaction and pride. Lizzie has a handkerchief and is ready to wave each time her sister will pass by.

"I wish Ma and Pa could see you now!"

I have to shout above the general clatter of feet moving on and off the wooden boards and in doing so I suddenly spy our sister Harriet being helped off one of the horses by a man, a stranger, not someone I can recognise. She is blissfully unaware of our presence, intent on gripping his arm, but what startles me most in seeing her climb down is the way her long coat hangs loose, and I am shocked by what I see. It begins to dawn on me why she has been so distant with us over the past few months, and I can only stand in mild disbelief at what I've seen, unable to think straight, merely watching as Harriet and the man get swallowed up into the crowd.

Albert has been noticing, too, in his usual quiet way and he senses my unease. We are still watching Mary having the ride of her life, her hair flying behind her each revolution, but he looks at me intently.

"She's not your problem, Flo, just forget about her tonight and try to enjoy yourself."

"I can't believe what I've just seen. It must be a mistake, all these confusing lights…"

"Now listen, Flo, I happen to know about that Jack-me-lad your sister was with. We've heard tell he's a rogue and after any young gal he can get. More fool your sister if she's after him. It'll all end in tears and more if what we've witnessed is true."

45

Although we go on to buy sticky toffee apples and all four of us share a dream boat ride, rocking us higher and higher, my laughter is not as genuine as theirs, and in spite of the fact I put on a brave face for Mary and Lizzie, inside me there is a feeling of disbelief and fear of the future for my sister Harriet.

Albert leads us homeward and gets us all singing a little song. I'm quite taken aback by his deep melodic baritone voice as I listen to the words. He seems to know a bit of the verse and charms us with it.

"But she married for wealth, not for love, he cried, though she lives in a mansion grand…"

This is our cue to join in as we heartily sing, "She's only a bird in a gilded cage, a beautiful sight to see!"

The chorus gets louder as near our homes and we suddenly hear a booming voice in the dark.

"Can't a chap get any peace these days? Off to your beds, you young varmints!"

I have to giggle, for we all recognise the gruff tones of old Mr Groom from the end cottage. We all offer our thanks to Albert.

"Thank you, Bertie, you've been very kind to us all."

I feel I should say more, but words won't come. However, I can still feel the warmth of his hand as he briefly touches mine as we part company.

Chapter 11
Winter

My life now follows a steady pattern of spending more time with Ophelia, often leaving Millie to cope with preparation of meals. The dreary month of November has kept us indoors, unable to go out on our little jaunts, but we've carried on with our painting sessions and taken to designing our own fashions. I think she has a good eye for colour and I try hard to imitate her with my drawings. We often sit chatting as if we were sisters, passing the time of day or reading aloud to each other. Ophelia can't wait until December and gets animated whenever she talks about the fun we'll have together at Christmas. I usually smile in agreement, but know all too well where I'd prefer to be: back at home. For as we reach the first day of December, my whole family are invigorated, in spite of the drab, cold and dark mornings when frost seeps through into our bones. We are buoyed up, knowing that in this countdown to the holy day of our Lord's birth, we too will be celebrating a succession of family birthdays, and any celebration, however small, is an occasion to be marked and cherished.

Our Lizzie always boasts that hers is far more important, as it falls on the first of the month. She starts to get excited a few days beforehand, but my brother Tom, whose birthday falls the day after hers, will always dampen her enthusiasm by chanting in his simple way, "First the worst! Second the best! First the worst! Second the best!"

"Shush, young Thomas! Don't tease your sister."

It saddens me to think what life has in store for him. Folk merely see a strapping lad of seventeen with dark, tousled hair, seemingly capable of anything, when in reality he is like a shadow man who drifts in and out of the real world, only able to do the most menial of tasks. Ma vehemently sticks up for her son, claiming he is the best chicken farmer in the world, and only then will you see Thomas grin as he hears those words.

Ma somehow always manages to scrape together enough ingredients to conjure up a small cake for us, but I don't think the stub of candle will last much longer as it gets continually used this month. Not that birthdays make any difference to our usual working lives, as we simply carry on with our normal tasks.

We had earlier been shaken from our sleep by our mother, although how she manages to be up so early, we cannot imagine. She tells us you have to bang your head upon the pillow a certain number of times and it will work, but it sadly fails when I try to do it. There is a basin of cold water standing on the chest that serves all us girls and jars us into action with its unwelcome chill.

"Happy birthday, our Lizzie."

I give her a huge squeeze as she hurriedly pulls on her skirt, then I delve into one of my pockets and hand her a small gift I have wrapped in some pretty blue paper I was allowed to take from the vicarage.

"I hope you like it. I made it especially for you!"

"Thanks, Flo. It looks very special! I shall open it when we get downstairs."

We descend the curving squeaky steps and are welcomed by smiling faces all eager to call out, "Happy Birthday Lizzie!"

Ma has done us each a boiled egg for a treat. She ushers her daughter on to her usual stool.

"Well, our Lizzie! A young lady of fifteen! How my little chicks are growing up fast! Your father and Henry have had to leave earlier, but he's put a little something by your plate from me and him."

Lizzie sees the little scrap of brown paper, feels it and knows instinctively that it will contain a shiny coin or two and that pleases her a lot. "You are so thoughtful, Ma. Thanks for that."

Jack and Thomas have been watching and listening, more intent on eating, but they too call out muffled birthday greetings from their bench further down the table.

There's no sign of Harriet who must have left earlier and we know that our eldest sister Sue does sometimes stay over at the farm.

Mary rushes in from using the outside privy, rubbing her hands vigorously to warm them after being out in the cold air. "Happy birthday to you! And I've got you something you'll love!"

"Let the poor girl eat up or both she and Flo will be late for work. What's in the pretty blue packet, I wonder?"

Ma looks on curiously as Lizzie unwraps my gift of a bag I had made whilst sewing with Ophelia.

"It's beautiful, Flo. How did you manage to make this?"

"The Reverend's daughter has been teaching me and she found some lengths of material I could use. I've made the long cord so you can wear it and feel safe."

"Open mine!"

Mary is hopping from one foot to another in eager anticipation of giving her gift. Lizzie takes the small package and unfurls a rather sticky toffee apple from its wrapper and laughs.

"Just what I needed Mary! How kind of you."

Lizzie hugs her in appreciation, but we must soon be on our way, so eating breakfast is the priority right now.

Reaching the crossroad, we part company after she has thanked me once again for her gift. As I walk briskly along the little lane, I relive the happy atmosphere of those breakfast moments and feel a great affection for my family, but now my thoughts must be upon today for I know I will be quite busy.

49

Reverend Henderson had hinted yesterday that they were expecting a visitor.

"Florence, I've a special favour to ask. Will you serve an early light lunch tomorrow? Our guest can only stay a short while: oh, and one of your delicious apple pies would be greatly appreciated by us all!"

Millie is hard at work as I enter the kitchen and the deep smell of baking greets me.

"I did the cheese scones all right this time, didn't I?"

I can see the plate she is pointing to and am quite impressed with her latest efforts. "We'll make a good cook of you yet, Millie. Good work. All the other things done this morning?"

"Yes, Miss Florence, all tidied, just like you says."

I love the warmth of any kitchen. It's where I feel most comfortable with what I know, for although I am called away on different occasions to be with Ophelia, the Reverend has accepted that I am an asset to his household and his particular love of good plain wholesome food. I'm grateful Ma has taught us girls the importance of a good meal to fill men's bellies, especially after a hard day's work. Not that the Reverend has hard manual work to do, but on days when he is out visiting folk in his extended parish, he can often return late in the evening, looking weary from all the walking. That's when he appreciates a good hot broth to revive his spirits.

Millie and I work well together and at the allotted time a bell is rung from the dining room. Millie sweeps back a few stray hairs beneath her little cap, rushing past me. With the door ajar, I can hear voices and laughter. There is a much deeper voice that weaves in and out of those outbursts and as I load the trays I become curious about this mystery guest. Millie rushes back into the kitchen.

"He says to have it now!" she blurts out.

I feel I need to correct her if she is ever to stay with us.

"Millie! You must call him the Reverend, and you must say they're ready for luncheon to be brought in!"

She takes no notice, shrugs her shoulders and repeats, "He said now!"

I pass her one of the trays, shaking my head in frustration and together we take the lunch into the dining room. The Reverend is in conversation with their visitor as I enter, but they turn their heads as Ophelia calls out then grabs my arm.

"This is my dear friend Florence! Come and meet Jean-Claude. He says he wants to know who has put all this happiness in my soul!"

Standing before me is a slender man, well dressed with a loosely tied golden cravat that looks very foreign to my eyes. His smile is hesitant but warm and he peers at me over a pair of fashionable spectacles, the like of which I've never seen before. I feel rather stupid standing there holding on to the tray.

"It is a pleasure to meet a friend of Ophelia and they are telling me you are the magician from the kitchen who feeds them so well! So I am Jean-Claude, and I shall be delighted to be taking the wonderful food you have prepared."

His foreign accent fascinates me and I offer a weak smile in return before extracting myself from Ophelia's arms whilst still balancing the tray. I now set it on the side dresser before transferring the dishes to the table. I'm all too aware of the strange looks this gentleman is giving me. He looks puzzled that I should be serving their lunch yet am hailed as Ophelia's friend. I guess he is confused about my position in this household. Ophelia looks so excited to be in his company and distracts him with her chatter. It pleases me to see how much more confident she has grown over the last months. Millie is still staring open mouthed at the visitor, quite entranced by his appearance. As I do not want to be drawn into further conversation, I usher her towards the door and we slip away before the grace is said. This continual feeling of being torn inside persists, the one half of me wanting so much to be a continual part of their lives, whilst the other part draws me back to where I know I really belong.

51

Chapter 12
Anticipation

It dawns on me that the forthcoming Christmas festivities are relished by everyone, be they rich or poor, for just as at home, there is similar activity at the vicarage with vigorous plans to prepare cakes and other traditional fare. Reverend Henderson has arranged for a freshly cut fir tree to be delivered, but not until Christmas Eve. Ophelia is so impatient she has already located the large wooden box that contains glass ornaments and trinkets for its decoration. It is in one of the store cupboards outside, near the porch. Today she has called me from the kitchen to help her move it indoors. Curiosity gets the better of me and I can't resist peeping inside as she raises the lid.

"Oh look, Florence! Won't it be fun when we can decorate the tree and make it shimmer and shine? Look, my dear mama made this one just for me."

Out of some tissue paper she pulls a pretty dark blue diamond made of satin that is embroidered with miniature roses that surround the letter O for her name. I can sense the love that had gone into the making of it and watch as Ophelia kisses it affectionately in remembrance. She hands it to me with a smile.

"Oh, it's really beautiful and a lovely memory of your dear mother, and what's more, I think you've inherited her talents for making and sewing."

It is satisfying that she no longer becomes tearful when we talk of such things and I smile at her as she takes back the treasured ornament and tucks it safely away. Although curious to see what other treasures will be inside, I will have to wait a little longer for that, but I do feel excited.

Back in the kitchen with my hands working hard at the dough, I reflect on the humbler way in which our cottage will be decorated for Christmas. We just have a few branches brought in and placed in a faded jug that belonged to Grandma. We tie on any coloured ribbons that we can find. Mary has been storing shiny acorns since the autumn, which we thread together and drape around, whilst Tom plays his part by making stars out of old newspapers. He can't work out how to fix them, so they tend to tear as he pushes them. Lizzie will always find the best one and secure it firmly at the topmost point. Even this modest attempt thrills us all as we await the final touches. Every Christmas Eve, Pa will come home with several brown packages and we just know what one of them will be! We are ordered to close our eyes tightly and not to peep, but we all know that he is tying white sugar mice by their tails on our tree, and we all shriek with feigned surprise. It reminds us of winter icicles and we love it, but now I am restless to help Ophelia decorate a proper tree as it promises to be an exciting event. I've only once seen a real one standing in the window of the Manor House in Felborough, all lit up and swathed with strings of fine beads, and it took my breath away.

For now I must press on, especially as Millie hasn't been well these last few days. She had caught a bad cold after one heavy downpour of rain, so the Reverend sent her home as she was shivering and shaking so much. So, I need to be busy and my precious time in the company of Ophelia has been limited. Yet I feel at peace in this kitchen where all is quiet and I can let my thoughts wander. I think about the other December birthdays that are still to come. I've been given permission to make a special treat for Ma's birthday in four days' time. It will be special for her as it falls on a Sunday, so I am planning to make sweetened bread filled with fruit in the shape of a heart, to show her how much I love her.

53

It's 13th December today and that means it is the birthday of my brother Joe. He is never fussed by this occasion in spite of the fact we tell him he looks quite the young gentleman at sixteen. He always grumbles that his falls on an unlucky day as nothing nice happens on the 13th. I think he gets embarrassed by the fuss we all make, as he only grabs a hunk of bread before rushing out. As it is, he'll be working long hours. New horses are being delivered and will need settling in at the stables, so he will not have time to enjoy his special day. I once heard him out in the scullery berating Ma for giving birth to five of us in the month of December. Being a girl, it didn't take much to work out that our parents were only taking advantage of the welcome break at Easter time. Sometimes I see how weary Ma has become having produced us in quick succession, plus the traumas of losing other babes throughout her life. Joe had taken his small cake from Ma and I hope he was also appreciative of the new shiny penknife she and Pa had given him.

Henry never did turn up for this his special birthday one week ago. There was no sighting of him at all. He had not come home the night before and Ma was somewhat disappointed. But she knows all too well his likeness for a drink or two at The King's Head in Felborough and has been told he frequently passes out. She fears he will take after his father now he has come of age, but will always worry about her firstborn. We've heard from friends that he has been seen around the town with a dark-haired girl. Ma wants to know more and hopes she is the type of lass that will get him back on a straight and sober path. I know she wants us all to be at home at Christmas time, but that may not be possible as I shall be needed elsewhere; I have been invited to share a meal at the vicarage. I've not plucked up the courage to tell Ma of my plans for fear of distressing her.

I still had not said anything by the Sunday of Ma's birthday, but vowed to do it before I left. We are woken in our chilly attic by an unusual brightness coming from the small window in the eaves. My sister Sue is back with us farm the farm and she leaps out to find out why. Still under my cover, I hear a squeaking sound and peer over the top to watch her rubbing frantically on the iced glass.

"Hey, look everyone! Old Jack Frost has been and I think it might have snowed overnight."

Pulling warm shawls around our bodies, we huddle together by the iced panes, each of us making peep holes to view the white world outside.

Mary is clearly disappointed. "It's only a white frost." She pouts at first, but then enthuses, "I bet the puddles will be all frozen over and they'll be great for sliding on! Come on, let's go outside and see!"

Lizzie is shivering and reminds us we had agreed to be up early to do the chores and thus spare Ma from working hard. We tiptoe down the rickety staircase, trying not to disturb our snoring brothers who have their bedding downstairs. Huddled in the scullery, Lizzie takes charge for once. I set to and light the fire beneath our copper, which in turn heats a small hot plate where Mary is setting up a large pan of porridge to cook. Lizzie orders a reluctant Sue to bring in the buckets of water stored by the back door. This is not an enviable task today with the film of ice to break. We are normally used to Harriet being the one in charge as the eldest girl, but she is not there this morning. I saw her briefly when she breezed in the cottage after her Saturday morning work, but all she did was to swiftly change her clothes and then call out as she was leaving.

"Jessie and me are going out tonight, Ma. There's a fellow who is coming to sing down at Wicks" Barn and we're going to listen to him. It might end quite late so I'm stopping over at her place, but I'll see you tomorrow. Bye."

Ma never got a chance to answer her, but had looked somewhat perplexed. I had watched Harriet as she moved to see if my suspicions still held true, but as she was wrapped in a thick coat, I was none the wiser. I sensed that her feeble tale about listening to a singer was far from the truth.

Lizzie is laying the table with spoons and placing our little secret packages alongside where Ma sits. Today we shall celebrate and treat Ma as if she is the Queen and then we shall insist she puts her feet up, because we know already that Pa has made her a new footstool as a surprise.

Chapter 13
Disturbing News

I'm relieved to see Millie back on Monday as there is much to do. We both feel very fortunate to have secure work in winter time, preparing food in the spacious vicarage kitchen, glad of its homely warmth against the cold winds that have started to blow across the fields. We make a good team now, and she has been a quick learner. Her batch of Christmas pies, crammed full with spicy fruits, were so tempting that when they were brought out of the oven that the Reverend couldn't resist tasting not one, but two, saying how delicious they were! I did feel very proud of Millie for her efforts, but those happy thoughts are swiftly banished at the sight of a distraught Miss Ophelia bursting into the kitchen and sobbing uncontrollably.

"Oh Florence! I don't know what to say!"

She rushes up to me and lays her head upon my shoulder, her body trembling as she cries. I lose all my inhibitions and clasp her tightly in my arms.

"Oh, my poor darling, whatever is troubling you? Now, just you sit down here and tell me what the problem is."

"It's just so unfair, I don't want to go!"

Her tear-streaked face looks up at mine and I see desperation in her eyes, and fear. I find myself reacting very swiftly.

"Millie, will you please carry on while I take Miss Ophelia into the parlour? And perhaps make a hot tea to help calm her down."

I whisper the last part, strip off my apron and gather my wits about me. I do not want Millie to witness any private confessions that may be about to be revealed and so gently encourage Ophelia to stand, her body still quivering with the sobs and together we walk out of the kitchen.

The parlour at the vicarage is a dark, chilly room. Its heavy curtains look worn and slightly frayed, but do keep the cold winds out when drawn. Today there is just a narrow opening, showing enough light for us to sit together. I'm thankful I have a clean folded handkerchief in my skirt pocket, which I do not hesitate to use as I gently wipe her face, uttering low soothing sounds to calm her.

"Sh, my dear, I'm sure whatever is troubling you can't be that bad. My own mama always says a trouble shared is a trouble halved, so now why don't you tell me what the problem is?"

Ophelia has calmed down a little, but looks very unhappy. "Oh Florence, where do I begin? I didn't want this to happen, just when things were going so well for us."

She fervently grips my hands in hers, the soulful eyes fixed upon my expectant face.

"Papa say we have to leave here at the end of the year and..."

She is unable to carry on, sitting there rocking herself to and fro as the tears flow once more. My instinct is to hold her tight, and then the reality of what she has just said begins to register. This could well spell the end of my current position, just when it looked like my world was all set to change. I pull away and Ophelia sits looking lost and forlorn. Her next action takes me by surprise as she suddenly flees from the room and I hear her footsteps racing up the staircase as she heads for the security of her bedroom.

I find myself rooted to my seat, myriad thoughts swirling in my head of what has occurred over the past six months, of my anticipated hopes and foolish dreams that seem to be crashing down before me. All the confidence I had mustered just a few moments ago has evaporated. With a very heavy heart I left the parlour, unsure of what to say when I return to the kitchen. Millie gives me a quizzical look as I return, but says nothing. I too am at a loss to speak, deciding instead to steer clear of any awkward conversation.

"Miss Ophelia has calmed down and is in her room. Nothing for you to worry about, Millie."

I can feel my stomach churning with anxiety and guilt at the untruths I have said, but I understand this news will also have consequences for Millie, too. I know that in the past there have been changes within the parish and new ministers have been brought in, so there is a glimmer of hope that both of us could be retained for the new incumbent and his family. With a firm resolve, I decide to speak with Reverend Henderson as soon as he is back. Right now, all I can do is focus upon lunch and try to pretend that all is well.

"You all right, Flo? You look a bit shook up after that carry on."

Unable to look her in the eye, I lie once more. "Just got the monthly belly ache, Millie."

She shrugs her shoulders and continues chatting as she peels the vegetables.

"My sister Elsie gets the gripes too, sometimes has to spend a day in bed, clutching a hot stone next to her for relief!"

With this diversion I am spared any more talk concerning the earlier outburst, but as I work I listen intently for the Reverend's returning footsteps.

I hear the heavy front door opening and closing just before one o'clock, which poses a dilemma as to whether I confront the issue or wait until after lunch is served. I decide then and there it will be the former option, so I head somewhat cautiously into the hall. Reverend Henderson is still removing his outer coat and turns to look at me. His face looks troubled and I sense he is pausing, not sure of what to say.

"Florence, I need to speak with you. Shall we say after lunch today? Nothing for you to worry about, my dear. Any sign of my daughter? She didn't seem too happy this morning."

He doesn't wait for me to answer, but heads towards his study and I'm left still wondering at what will eventually be said. By now my stomach really does ache and I feign such discomfort that Millie is ordered to take in the lunch with instructions to say as little as possible.

So, this is the moment I've been dreading. Reverend Henderson invites me to take one of his study chairs whilst he sits, his elbows on the desk and hands propping beneath the greying beard.

"I feel rather sad having to say this, Florence, and it's a very hard thing to do, but I have just received orders from the Bishop to vacate this parish in the New Year and head for pastures new in Shropshire. Now I can't stress what a splendid help you've been to both myself and my daughter and for that I am deeply grateful. It saddens us both when we have become part of this friendly village, but I must go where I can best serve our Lord. I realise this means a change in your current position."

I sit there as if frozen in time, the reality of his words leaving me in a turmoil of emotions as I dread what he will next say.

He hesitates before adding, "Unfortunately you will not be needed here when the next family move in, but I am able to tell you that on my recommendation I have spoken highly of your talents and if you so desire, a place is available for you in the kitchens at Branswick Hall. We shall be sorry to leave this lovely area and the gentle folk of the parish, and most of all, yourself. I do hope you understand, Florence. Now, I'd like you to go and find my daughter, who is a little heartbroken that she will be leaving such a good friend behind."

I am at a loss to answer, and merely nod my head in some sort of acknowledgement whilst stifling tears that are threatening to blur my vision. As I leave the study I can only think of those exciting times when I'd imagined my life was going to change for ever, the little jaunts Ophelia and I had experienced, the personal times we had shared confidences, now to be faded memories of what might have been. It is with a heavy heart I go searching for her, unsure of what I will do or say.

Chapter 14
Finality

These final days pass without meaning for me and my work at the vicarage seems like a penance, all the expectation of festivities now dulled by the tearful moods of Ophelia and my own disappointment that life would be taking me in a different direction, one I can foresee of mere drudgery. Yet I have no other option than to accept the offer of work at Branswick Hall. I was told it was all prearranged and that I was to report to Mrs Baynton the housekeeper at 7.30 on 2nd January. I feel rather guilty, as it seems so unfair on Millie, who will be out of work and was not offered an alternative. Oddly, she doesn't seem to be bothered.

"My sis says she'll put in a word for me up the big hotel near the station. She reckons they always need help, and anyway, I fancy a change."

I'm envious of Millie's optimism, but think her somewhat naive in her expectations of working in the kitchens. I have a friend who finally managed to secure a humble position there as a laundry maid, and I heard how strict their inspections were for new staff.

Ophelia still begs me to join her, but it doesn't seem right any longer to be so familiar with her. I've kept myself to the kitchens to avoid her demands. However, today I have sat with her in the library. All around there are signs that some of the precious volumes have already been stowed in stout boxes.

"Dearest Florence, I'm going to miss you so much when we move away. But you must promise to write to me and who knows, we might someday meet again."

In my heart I would wish that, too, but know those words are in vain. I feel I need to praise her and bolster her self-esteem.

"Ophelia, you have been a great friend and I've been privileged to be with you on our little outings. I can't thank you enough and I believe your darling mama would be have been so proud of the kindness you have shown me."

She reaches out to hold my hands and I feel choked inside with our shared disappointment. A brief smile breaks out on her sad pale face.

"But we shall still have a tree being delivered tomorrow, although I think Papa has said it must be a small one. I insist you decorate with me!"

Her enthusiasm is infectious and I nod my acceptance, for this might be the only chance I ever get. I cannot bear to think how painful it will be when we finally part, so I am determined to enjoy this last little pleasure.

It is quite dark when I head for home, and even though the route is familiar I feel my way along, keeping to the side whilst carefully stepping to avoid the deep ruts formed by cart wheels. As I reach the crossroads, I can make out the familiar shadow of someone and hear the ring of a bell. I hope with all my heart it is Albert and am so grateful to see him there, leaning against his bicycle.

"You made me jump, Albert! Now why are you waiting here? Have you forgotten which way to go?"

I can't resist teasing him and I don't really need him to explain, as he has done this once before to surprise me.

"Because I'm a perfect gentleman and I'm just waiting for the perfect lady to escort her home!"

His infectious grin lifts my spirits and I am truly grateful for his company right now. We walk a little way in silence and I feel brave enough to share my sad news with him. He must have been thinking about what to say for we both start speaking together, then chuckle when we realise what has happened.

63

"After you, Miss Gibbs!"

I quite like the soft way in which he speaks to me, but am startled to hear him say, "Word's going around that there vicar of yours is leaving and it set me a-wondering."

I should have known there are no secrets in a small village like ours and that such news was bound to be widely known, although I doubt if my Ma or sister Lizzie would have spoken out. I had been grateful to find just the two of them sitting sewing when I returned home with the news that fateful day. It was so hard to tell them that I would shortly be leaving the vicarage. However, I was able to reassure Ma that I would still be in service, but living in. Naturally they had shared in my disappointment. Ma seemed rather cross and insisted I was to be at home for Christmas Day, which still posed a dilemma for me as I did not want to offend the Reverend. Right now I am aware that Albert is gazing silently at me as we walk together, his pale blue eyes watching me in a concerned way. I nod my head, choosing my words carefully.

"Nothing lasts for ever, and you've heard right, Albert. The Reverend has to move on. That's just the way it is, but I don't have to worry because he has kindly fixed it for me to be working up at the Hall. Now, isn't that a grand opportunity!"

I make it sound like an exciting adventure so as to allay his fears, but do not reveal that I won't be around for a while. The thought of having to live in seems like a prison sentence to me, but I have no choice.

With a heavy heart I try to keep as cheerful as I can as the days tick past. I busy myself with cooking, as that way it takes my mind off the changes that will take place in January. After much deliberation I have spoken to the Reverend saying that I am needed at home on Christmas Day, thanking him for his kind offer of dining with them but assuring him that Millie is more than capable of preparing and serving their meals that day.

The early morning arrival of the fir tree on Christmas Eve causes a flurry of excitement amongst us all. It has been placed in a large ceramic bowl and taken into the dining room, where the wonderful smell from the needles fills the room. Ophelia demands I join her that very instant and I am determined carry out this last pleasurable activity with her. She delves into the wooden box that holds the little ornaments and urges me to do the same.

"Oh, this is so exciting. I almost forgot how many of these glass baubles there are. Look, Florence! Aren't they wonderful?"

I've never seen anything so delicate before and am fearful I might break them. Inside the box I see several fabric toys, miniature dolls and soldiers, along with some sweet little felt hearts. Each one has a delicately sewn pattern of tiny sequins or raised embroidery and I strongly suspect they are the fine workmanship of her late mother.

"Perhaps if you do the glass ones, Ophelia, I can make a start with these."

I savour every moment of this satisfying task, seeing the plain tree come alive with colour. Reverend Henderson stops by and admires our handiwork and has to insist he be the one to place the fragile Angel Gabriel on the highest branch. It looks very old to me and has a tendency to lean at an odd angle, however much we then try to straighten it. Finally, and with much love, Ophelia hangs the blue diamond in the centre, taking pride of place. I think it looks magical, but discover there is still more to add.

"Now, there are some candles, but Papa refuses to let them be lit for fear we burn down the room, but they will still look jolly in their holders if we clip them on here, just like this, on the very ends of the branches!"

I know I shall never forget this day as we stand back to view our joint efforts and vow that in future years, I shall try and do the same to keep a similar tradition alive. Before I return to the kitchen, Ophelia takes me to one side. I can see she is hesitating, unsure of what to say. After a deep breath she begins.

"It is going to be so difficult saying our goodbyes next week, for I know I will end up crying and unable to say the right things to you. Dear Florence, I shall miss you dreadfully and by way of thanking you I insist you accept the dresses I have given you as a reminder of the happy times we shared. I'll never forget..."

Her words trail off as she rushes out of the room, choked up with emotion. It's then the finality of my situation really hits me hard.

Chapter 15
February

"Come on gal, sharpish! His Lordship will be waiting for that tray!"

The housekeeper shoots a menacing glare at me, her eyes widening with threat as she deliberately edges nearer. Without need of a second warning, I grip the heavy tray firmly and turn quickly through the doorway, my heart rate rising with fear of the unknown. Almost two months have passed since my arrival here at Branswick Hall, two long monotonous months of hard work and disillusionment as the promise of a position in the kitchens only transpires to be that of a humdrum skivvy, working much longer hours and hating every moment. Right now, I've been tasked to cover for one of the serving maids who is ill, so this will be the first time I've left the kitchen for any duty and I can feel myself quivering with nervous anticipation as I begin to negotiate the rather tight curves of the back stairwell. At the top I pause to take some deep breaths to brace myself for the next unknown situation. I mentally go over the words my mother said when I had left home on that chilly January morning.

"You just remember, gal, they ain't no better than us, just got a load more money. Keep your thoughts to yourself, and smile that lovely smile the good Lord gave you, lass. You know what I mean?"

Buoyed by those thoughts, I find myself two floors up and as per directed, I follow the corridor looking intently for the morning room. The tray is quite heavy, so I have to hold it firmly for fear of dropping it, but I glance at the ornate doorways on each side intersected with the most delicate china figurines that stand upon highly polished half tables the like of which I've never seen before. Ahead of me now are a pair of heavily studded doors and I pray silently that I have reached the right room. Carefully balancing the tray, I knock rather timidly, whereupon one door is opened by an officious-looking manservant. He almost snatches the tray from me with a look of disdain that I've often witnessed towards the lower ranks of staff. I scan the opening and can see Lord Gressingham himself, reading a newspaper and sitting in what only looks like a sunburst of glorious colour, his five unkempt hunting dogs at his feet. He jerks his head and stares at me, so I decide to bob a discreet curtsey and begin to back away.

"Come here, girl!"

His deep booming voice startles me, then as the servant is about to close the door I notice I am being beckoned to enter the room.

"Let her come in, Withers."

I am overwhelmed by the grandeur of a room that is the largest I've ever been in. Now I know why it's called the Golden Room. To me it feels like a palace. I've never seen anything so grand before. I can't help but fleetingly remember that one exhilarating time I had been with Ophelia in one of the wings of the Hall. At the time even that impressive space had felt so grand and spacious, but this fair takes my breath away. I step gingerly forward, feeling the disapproving glare from the servant who now stands in pompous attention behind His Lordship's chair.

"Name?"

I hesitate following that command, aware of the crackling logs upon the fire and a plaintive whine from one of the Irish wolfhounds, for I find my mouth dry and incapable of speech.

Then in in more friendly way he adds, "You must be new here. Now, what shall I call you?"

My fear abates and I find myself answering with a second curtsey.

"I'm called Florence, sir."

There, I've said it. Why shouldn't I? My boldness has returned and I remember my manners and smile at him. There is an explosion of laughter as he leans back in the faded leather armchair. Then with the twist of his hand he motions in a spiral movement for me to turn around. Now I do feel awkward at this strange request. I liken it to when my Uncle Henry exhibits his prize cattle at the county shows.

I feel emboldened to challenge his command and rather outspokenly I blurt out, "I'm not here for dancing, sir!"

I can already feel my face redden with embarrassment and the stupidity of my words, knowing I have spoken out of turn but to my surprise His Lordship looks highly amused and is chuckling to himself.

"So it's Florence, is it? A Florence with a lively spirit, I see! Well, well, Florence always has a special place in my heart. Don't you agree, Withers? Those lovely summers in Italy, heady days in the Tuscan sun."

I am a little bemused by comments that I do not quite understand, for I only know that Italy is on a map shaped like a boot.

"Florence, I shall expect to see your smiling face up here every morning. That's all. Off with you!"

Stunned at his words, I watch as he sinks behind the newspaper again and Withers is all too keen to lever me out of the sumptuous room. As the door closes behind us, he hisses a warning to me before returning to his duties.

"Keep your lips buttoned in future! And no cheek to His Lordship in future!"

Stepping carefully as I descend the stairwell, I feel a certain satisfaction at this encounter, although I'm still amazed at the way I had responded. When I had first come here, I was welcomed in some small way by my cousin Annie who showed me how things worked. She has been here for two years, so was well placed to give me good advice as to how I was meant to fit in. It was so unnerving after the joyful months I had so enjoyed at the vicarage, but I had to dismiss those ideals as lost for ever and now obey commands, in particular those of the housekeeper who still spends her time watching us kitchen staff, ever eager to find fault with all and sundry. At least when I'm working it is alongside others and that can give me a warm feeling of friendship. I am still learning how to use some rather weird kitchen gadgets. There's a spiral machine for peeling apples, but I think I could do it just as efficiently by hand.

Mrs Baynton is still hovering by the long dresser at the side of the kitchen as I enter the room. There is no word of thanks, but a barked statement.

"You had better wipe that smile off your face, and don't expect to be doing that again. Back to your work."

We are the nameless ones down here, only meriting our given due when we have excelled at some dish or other. I'm used to it now, so bury my head, keep silent and begin tackling the large mound of potatoes.

Sometimes I miss living at home, all the lively family jesting that occurs around the kitchen table. There has only been one occasion when I have been able to pass on a note to let them know I am well. I do not reveal my true unhappiness as I do not want to distress Ma. It was fortunate that one morning I recognised the carrier as Ben, who delivers back in High Weldon and he seemed agreeable to pass on my letter when he next called. But there is never a return message and each day I wonder how they are all doing. My chief concern is what has happened to Harriet.

Only two days ago, I happened to be outside in the yard, having been ordered to take a small basket across to the stables for the head groom, when I was stunned to see my eldest brother Henry standing there, happily chatting to him. Now I know Henry works chiefly up in the woods so it was a little surprising to see him there. They were joshing around at some joke and Henry threw back his head and laughed out loud, before spotting me as I stood rooted to the ground. Would he speak to me, I wondered, or should I interrupt their banter?

Thankfully he gestured to the groom with a wave of his hand and walked over to me.

"Our little Flo! I'd forgotten what a fine young lady you've turned out to be! Now why the troubled looks, eh?"

I was too concerned to ask after his welfare, but I needed to know:

"Have you seen Harriet lately?"

As soon as I'd said this, I felt a fool. How would he know when his work keeps him from being part of our family life? Henry had gripped my elbow steering me towards the wall.

"You ought to know Flo, she's gone. We don't know where and Ma's frantic about it all. Nobody has seen her for over a month. Dad has had men out looking for her around the fields and in the ditches, but it's like she's vanished into thin air. I'm sorry to have to tell you, Flo, but there's nothing we can do about it. Now, I'd better be shooting back before I gets into trouble for hanging around the big house."

My blank face must have said it all, for Henry had a brief moment to hug me before leaving the yard with some haste, almost as if he did not wish me to see the tears welling in his eyes.

Chapter 16
Orders

I still live in dread of the housekeeper Mrs Baynton, who seems critical of my every move. I just apply myself to whatever job I'm given so that each day passes quickly. The cold weather persists and as February ends, spirits are very low for everyone in the household. This year has brought us many wet snow drifts that have kept the yard lads constantly sweeping them to the side, thus creating lasting puddles over which we have to step; my boots seem perpetually damp with rarely a chance for them to dry out. Tempers are rife with frustration and I've learned just to keep my mouth shut and not get drawn into any arguments with fellow staff. The only light relief I experience is having the opportunity to see the elaborate rooms upstairs and to know I'm fulfilling my duty to His Lordship, albeit for the briefest of moments. As I have to live in, it often feels like an imprisonment, unable to escape apart from the one day a month I am allowed to make the long trek home.

On my first visit back home in January it was like a day of birthdays, Christmas and Easter all rolled into one as my excitement rose at the thought of seeing my family again, albeit dampened slightly by the long fraught walk through the icy lanes back to Higher Weldon. Those few precious hours had brightened my spirits as we had supped and laughed together. Jack had been eager to show me his recent wood carvings, all from fallen branches, and I had to admire the clever way he had created delicate swans or little mice, and he had made a small owl especially for me! I felt very touched by this small token and rather guilty I had thought so little about them all since being away.

Lizzie seemed a lot happier. I learned that Mr Graves had been taken ill and needed nursing, so the shop had been put in the charge of one of his nieces. Lizzie said she was much nicer to work for. Ma looked weary, but her face lit up when I walked through the back door and she bundled me in her enveloping way, her strong arms holding me tight for what seemed ages. Thomas grinned in recognition but greeted me as Sue, and I had to remind him several times that I was Flo. His preoccupation that day was reorganising the pile of logs kept in a wooden bucket and muttering about how his chickens were not laying. Mary was her usual bundle of joy, eager to show me her scrapbook where she had been flour-pasting cut-out newspaper items showing all manner of buildings and scenes from foreign lands. My other brothers were not there, but that was quite normal, with Henry working up in the woods and Joe busy grooming and caring for the horses up at the Hall stables.

I had anticipated seeing my other two elder sisters, but very little had been said as to their whereabouts. Pa had managed briefly to call by on one of his rounds taking wood down to another part of the estate and he made us all jump as he stuck his reddened face around the door with a loud "Boo!"

With the door ajar and cold air entering, I thought he was coming in, but he hovered there instead. I sensed he was already showing the signs of having had an early drink and felt sad for Ma who would have to deal with his wild unruly nature later that night.

"And there's my bonny Flo! Still got a smile for your old dad?"

I forced the biggest grin I could muster, although seeing him troubled me somewhat and I think we felt relieved when he gave us a cursory wave and left. Ma moved to click the door tightly shut against the sharp wind that was blowing up another storm.

"Same old Dad! At least he's still working, Ma. I suppose you don't see much of Harriet and Sue with their jobs?"

I thought by wording it that way, I might find out any present news.

To our surprise, Tom suddenly yelled out in the most coherent way. "You won't see Sue 'cos he be up the farm and you won't see Harriet 'cos she be in the shoe factory. And you won't see me 'cos..."

This sudden revelation had left him speechless, but we all clapped to show how proud we were of his outpouring. Nothing more was said on this matter. Ma plied me with hot food, and it was so welcoming with the others fussing over me that I just enjoyed the moment, however short.

Trudging back as the light was fading fast, I started to think about Harriet and came to the conclusion that I had simply imagined her predicament. I felt content having seen most of them, so clutching the bag of buns Ma had pressed into my hands, along with my precious little owl, I felt good about myself again, even though my legs were very tired from the long road back to the Hall.

I wake with a feeling of sadness as I know that today will be the last day I am needed to take up the tray, now His Lordship's staff have recovered their health. Having glimpsed the world upstairs, I like what I see and feel that this is what I need to aim for. Mrs Baynton is looking angry this morning as I enter the kitchen. I had hoped she would at least thank me for my efforts, but her sharp words come as a complete surprise.

"God knows why, but I have received orders that you are to continue to take up the breakfast tray to Lord Gressingham every morning from now on. I shall expect you to maintain a dignified presence and return down here immediately to resume your kitchen duties. He requires it in his study this morning."

She sounds annoyed and mutters under her breath as she storms off. But this is very welcome news for me, for it affords me further glimpses of the grand life and my spirits are lifted. I happily take the tray and make my way up the stairs.

His Lordship is usually seated in his grandiose room, but there is no sign of him around. Withers is always hovering with a critical look on his face and he orders me to carry the breakfast tray into a smaller adjacent study. It contains huge tables strewn with large maps that curl over and have to be held in place by large books. The room is empty, so having placed the tray on the side table I can't resist having a good look around. Bookshelves are floor to ceiling, but they look too neatly stacked with all manner of matching volumes, as if they are just for show, and I notice that many titles seem quite illegible from the faded covers. There is a dark wooden writing bureau, firmly locked but with the key still in its shiny brass keyhole. However, my focus is drawn towards the paintings on the wall on each side. I can't but help admire them as one looks very familiar to me. It takes me back to that enlightening day when I had accompanied Miss Ophelia to this very same hall to admire the homely scenes painted by our local artist. I find myself gasping as I recognise one that features geese and ducks outside a picturesque flower covered cottage, and am so engrossed looking closely at it that I am totally unaware that Lord Gressingham has entered the room, closing the door behind him.

"Ah, Florence! I see you are admiring my works of art! And which one do you like the best?"

"Please don't be offended, sir. I was just admiring this particular picture."

There's something about being in his presence that encourages me to speak brazenly and freely without the presence of Withers, who tends to keep a close watch on my every movement. I feel more at ease as I see him peer closer to the painting.

"Yes, one of my latest acquisitions. Some new artist fellow who is acclaimed by one and all. So what do you like about it then, Florence?"

I take a deep breath, think hard and find myself saying, "I just love the way Mr Standard paints the birds, sir, and it's as if they are about to fly out of the picture."

I am taken aback as he shakes his head and laughs out loud. "Well, you do surprise me! I begin to wonder what other hidden talents you possess, young lady."

Holding his gaze, I chance a smile that might just leave him pondering upon that question, make a short curtsey and take a step backwards in readiness to leave, only to hear him add, "Incredible! I shall have to keep my eye on you, young lady!"

Fearing I might have said too much again, I give a curt bob and swiftly turn to leave, but with a warm feeling of satisfaction and pride that my life has turned for the better.

Chapter 17
March

"So, now I understand we have to call you *Florence* at His Lordship's request."

Mrs Baynton sneers as she stresses my name. I have just entered the kitchen, clad in my dark dress plus a new, crisp, white-frilled apron. Considering that up to now she has refrained from ever calling me Flo, I find her comment rather pointless. She turns to rearrange the fine cut glasses upon the dresser to deliberately snub me, but can't resist snapping at me.

"But just you remember when you're down here, you'll still be Flo, understand?"

Two of the other kitchen maids stifle a giggle and she duly reprimands them before continuing.

"I've got my eye on you, young madam. Your duties will be only to serve His Lordship at breakfast and then I expect you straight back down here. Is that clear?"

I hold my nerve and in a polite and clipped manner I answer, "Perfectly understood, Mrs Baynton."

The coolness of my deliberated response has obviously unnerved her and she speeds from the room and I breathe a sigh of relief. Maisie, the head cook, grins at me whilst she busies herself stirring a cake mixture.

"Don't you fret, me duck. I expects you was baptised Florence anyway, am I right? Tek no notice of Mrs B. Her bark's worse than her bite. After all, it were her that put you up for the job 'cos she could see you was a capable lass."

Staff don't often get to talk, so I am thankful for those few words of encouragement, even though I doubt they are true. Something tells me Mrs Baynton had been commanded to obey a request from higher up and is none too pleased to have to comply.

As the days are slowly warming, the prospect of spring around the corner has cheered us all up and I feel more settled than before. I'm counting the days until I get leave to visit home again, but even seeing the array of daffodils that have just sprung up in the flowerbeds fills me with happiness. The tray is all ready for me to carry and I head towards the curving staircase, balancing it with great care but with a greater confidence and poise. I now head steadily towards the oak door of the grand room and knock twice. I hear footsteps and Withers is there to open it. This morning he simply looks me up and down with a blank stare and thankfully has no scathing words, so I boldly step forward and place the tray myself upon the table that I am detailed to use.

There is no sign of either Lord Gressingham or his hunting dogs, just a blazing fire and some books and papers strewn carelessly upon the floor near his armchair. I hesitate for just a second or two, absorbing the warmth and admiring the large portraits hanging on each side of the fireplace. I half expect a barked order of dismissal from Withers, but he simply stands staring out of the large window that overlooks the grand driveway of the Hall. My curiosity gets the better of me and I work out I can leave the room by circuiting another chair in the vague hope I too can catch a glimpse of the activity. Sounds rising from below seem to indicate that a carriage has just drawn up, coupled with the sound of dogs barking, but all I can see as I pass behind Withers is the top of the driver's tall hat. I am none the wiser as I let myself out of the Golden Room.

I allow myself to stroll casually back, taking note of the odd passages that seem to lead from the staircase. As I near the base, I am particularly intrigued by an opening I've never noticed before. It is framed by an elaborate carved stone archway. My curiosity is aroused and, as I hear no one else around, I can't resist walking through to discover what is beyond. It feels cold, with a musty, damp smell. I'm eager to investigate further, daring myself to negotiate the dark, narrow turns. Then the corridor lightens as I come across a window in a recess that looks out into the grand courtyard entrance. This is quite exciting and I eagerly lean forward in the hopes of seeing more, but to no avail.

Many of the glass panes are darkened, and there is only one section where I can look through. It is on a level where I can only see the wheels of the carriage that arrived earlier, several dark clad legs that pass by, and I can hear the impatient pawing of horses' hooves. Then as I strain to see more, the atmosphere changes and I feel a sudden chill, as if I have been wrapped in an icy cold blanket. It feels as if someone has passed through me and now my heart rate has shot up with fear, beating so loudly it scares me as I stand frozen to the spot. Even the light has faded from the obscured window panes, and I am unable to make any sense of this feeling.

A deep voice startles me back to reality as an order is shouted out in the courtyard and I am desperate to retrace my steps, stumbling with fear and taking the deepest of breaths to steady myself as I leave the menacing corridor. Back at the base of the spiral stairwell, I have to pause in an attempt to calm my nerves and ready myself to appear back in the kitchen as if nothing untoward has happened. For a brief moment I attempt to rationalise what I had just experienced. Ah yes, I clearly recall how some of the staff had teased me when I had first come to the Hall. One of the junior cooks warned me about the resident ghost who was known to haunt the east wing, and Sidney, one of the cheeky younger stable lads, had been eager to scare me by telling me of the apparitions that were known to occur in the cellars. I had dismissed these taunts as mere folklore passed down to all newcomers. Right now, I must push all this nonsense clean out of my head, compose myself as if I had just this minute returned from my duties, and make myself walk as calmly as I can, with my legs still trembling, to face the rest of the day.

Chapter 18
Inspection

Back in the kitchen I half expect to be challenged over the time I have taken, but nothing is said. I discard my apron and fold it safely away before grabbing the working one. There are birds to be prepared and I'm glad of the monotonous distraction to forget what has so recently occurred. I'm also grateful for the welcome warmth radiating from the ovens as my hands tingle back to life. I don't object to hard work, but there are times when I feel torn inside, a sadness that my expectations were dashed when my position at the vicarage came to an abrupt end. It was as if I had been living a double life, and in my vanity, I was increasingly drawn to its grandeur and the opportunities it had thrown up. Yet it had been a shameful secret that I could never fully share with my dear family. I sigh to myself, still dreaming of what might have been, wondering how Ophelia is faring in her latest home. Mrs Baynton leaves us working and heads for the corridor. Maisie now takes advantage of her absence and starts chatting animatedly.

"It's His Lordship's sister, Lady Louisa. Chambers told me she's a bit weird, and that's why she's come here for the country air, not that I'd want to go out in this blooming cold air. You'd only go and get a sniffy cold if you did that!"

Maisie rhythmically kneads the dough, stressing every other word.

"And you should see the list I got given! Nothing with eggs "cos they bring her out in a rash, and could I get some asparagus as that's her favourite. Well, I ask you! Asparagus at this time of year; I don't think so!"

I have to smile at the way Maisie carries on, but these little outbursts are short lived when we are under scrutiny by our superior. You can see the kitchen staff go on high alert when the housekeeper returns with a purposeful look on her face. I'm rather glad I am standing just behind her so I don't fall under her austere glare. With two short claps of the hand she summons us.

"I have an important message from Lord Gressingham. He has invited his sister, the honourable Lady Louisa, to stay here at the Hall."

I catch the knowing look in Maisie's eyes, and can almost hear her thinking, "Oh we know that already!"

"You will pay special attention to the menus that she will require, in addition to those we normally prepare. And now there is one other thing."

She swings around to confront me, with a look of contempt as if loath to speak.

"You are to go into the library. I've no idea why, but that's the orders I've been given. Look sharp, girl! Remove your apron. Withers is waiting outside to take you there."

My heart is in my mouth, and I just know I'm going to be in trouble. As I meekly follow Withers in silence through new corridors I've never seen before, I berate myself for my earlier actions and wonder who has reported me for trespassing. I brace myself for the worst.

I am led into the library, which is so much bigger than the one I had known at the vicarage. There are two other girls standing in the centre of the room whispering to each other, but I do not know them, and begin to wonder if they too are here to be reprimanded. They do not speak, but look distinctly baffled at my presence in the room. My hands feel hot and sweaty as I attempt to formulate some mad excuse as to why I went exploring, but there is no further time to think, as Lord Gressingham sweeps into the room followed by the swirl of a taffeta skirt and the pale drawn face of a strange lady who I believe must be the new visitor spoken of downstairs.

"Over there! Stand up! Show your hands!"

The three commands are bellowed aloud by His Lordship and I move meekly to stand between the other two girls on one side of the library. There is just time to discreetly rub my damp hands on my skirt to dry them. Then as we obligingly stretch out our palms it feels as if we are to be chastised like in our school days. I lived in fear of one school master who revelled in slapping our palms with a wooden ruler if we misbehaved. Maybe this is one of the peculiarities of His Lordship and his way of punishing us.

"All yours, my dear Louisa. Ask away!"

To my utter astonishment, it dawns on me that we are being inspected and my previous fears are groundless, but as to why I have no idea at all.

"You are…?"

The question is aimed for the first girl who gives a very low curtsey before confidently replying, "Grace, Your Ladyship."

Nothing is said, but Lady Louisa inspects the outstretched palms, touching them with one ungloved hand before moving in front of me. I see a troubled face, with sad eyes staring at me so I do what comes naturally and give the friendliest smile I can and stretch out my hands.

"Your name?"

The two words are tentatively spoken. "I'm called Florence, Your Ladyship."

Then I curse myself for not making a curtsey, but stand there fascinated as she strokes my warm hands, a glimmer of a faint smile beginning to appear, but she still remains silent. The process is repeated with the last girl who looks a lot older than me. She appears more confident in replying and gives a curt little bob of respect.

"Jane, Your Ladyship. It would be an honour to serve you."

She looks quite smug as she speaks, clearly vying for attention.

Lady Louisa looks deep in thought, then walks towards her brother and we hear the faintest of whispers as he nods his head in some sort of approval then they both turn to face us.

"Jane and Grace, you may leave us now. Florence, please step over here."

This is it. This is the panic moment when I realise my trespassing has been found out and I feel extremely afraid, but in truth I still have absolutely no idea what is happening. I keep my head bowed as I await my fate. I listen as the library door is clicks shut and footsteps fade away. It comes as a total shock when I hear what His Lordship has to say.

"We think you will be suitable as a maid to assist my sister Lady Louisa for the time she stays here. Is that agreeable, Florence?"

I can't believe what I'm hearing! This is Lord Gressingham asking me if I mind! I can barely contain myself with this most unexpected feeling of elation and pride, so it is with a new enthusiasm I hold my head high and proudly say, "It will be an honour to serve you, Your Ladyship, and I'm happy to do whatever you bid me to."

Lady Louisa seems not to want to speak, but I observe her twisting her one free glove in an agitated manner suggesting to me she is of a nervous disposition, and rather in awe of her authoritarian brother. Lord Gressingham takes control of the situation, rubbing his hands together.

"Splendid! Now, off you go and get acquainted!"

It shocks me to hear him speak so bluntly, so I keep my eyes firmly fixed on her pallid face as if willing her to speak if only to show some approval and seal this unexpected turn of events. Finally, my warm smile at Her Ladyship elicits a response.

"I promise I won't send you away, or frighten you."

She is briskly interrupted by Lord Gressingham. "Now, now, none of that nonsense, all forgotten."

He steers his sister towards the library door and with one hand waves me to follow her.

"Take no notice of my sister's little outbursts. She's a delicate soul, but I feel confident you will be of great assistance to her during her stay with us."

And with that I am bid to follow the swishing dress, towards the blue wing and down a long corridor, where I glimpse all manner of elaborate blue and white oriental vases, the likes of which I've never seen before. I find myself in the grandest of bedrooms, almost lost for words at the sheer beauty of it all. Everything has happened in such a whirl I cannot believe my good luck. I know nothing about being a maid or what will be expected of me, but I am eager to learn and realise this is my one opportunity to rise to the occasion and make something of myself.

Chapter 19
New Horizons

That first day I was thrust unceremoniously into my new life was very demanding. I had to muster all my nerve to convince myself I could do as bidden, but I was at a loss to know where to begin and faced with an unknown lady who baffled and intrigued me. Once inside Her Ladyship's boudoir, I observed a complete change in her character that all started with the biggest of sighs as she pulled off her other glove and flung them both carelessly on to the dressing table.

"William is such a bore and fusses over me too much. I don't need to be helped but he would insist. Now, remind me what I call you?"

I start to see there is another side to this fretful lady, one I aim to understand and help.

"I am called Florence, M'Lady." This time I remember to bob courteously.

"Oh no, none of that nonsense! Your other name, girl?"

The sudden sharpness of her tone startles and agitates me and now I feel puzzled, unable to assess her true character.

"Gibbs, M'Lady."

"Well, Gibbs, what can you do for me?"

At first, I am at a loss on how to answer, for this is going to be a big departure from my earlier kitchen status and I still feel unsure if I will cope. I need to do some very quick thinking, based on the tales I have previously heard about the tasks demanded of their servants by the gentry. Well, I had some previous insight into their ways during my treasured time spent with Miss Ophelia, and my own family upbringing has taught me many life skills, so surely it can't be that different applying those to this new situation. Anyway, my role is to obey her commands, whatever they prove to be.

"I will carry out any duty you ask of me to my best ability. I am willing to learn and be guided by you, M'Lady."

Her reactions catch me completely unawares, as she flops inelegantly on to her bed, then bursts into laughter as her head falls on the colourful counterpane.

"They call me mad, you know! Mad Louisa! Sent me to this ghastly place for my health. Simpson couldn't bear to be with me any longer and so you are to take her place. You poor thing!"

Those last three stressed words sound almost threatening. I can only assume the Simpson she has referred to is a former personal maid and do wonder how true her words mean. These revelations begin to build a picture of this unconventional lady and I hope in the fullness of time, I will come to understand her emotional outbursts.

"So, shall it be Gibbs or do I emulate my brother and call you Florence? He's always had an eye on the pretty girls who work here! Didn't you wonder why you were chosen? His suggestion, of course."

I sense she is trying to shock me, or even suggest that there will could more to this unconventional arrangement, but I do not flinch, although my heart skips a beat when she shouts out.

"Oh why, oh why did I allow myself to be brought here? I shall just die of boredom!"

By now she is sitting up and I see part of her long greying hair has come adrift, so I use my initiative and take the ornate silver hairbrush from the table. It isn't the easiest of tasks with Her Ladyship perched at the foot of the bed, but I lean over and soon the repeated strokes have their calming effect as I brush and then rearrange the stray hair for her, pinning it in coils to match the other side. I think of the many times I have done the same to my sisters when at home and that sudden unexpected thought catches me off guard and I can feel a tightness in my throat at the memories and a wetness starting to blur my vision. I turn my head to the side, not wishing to be seen, and walk over to replace her hairbrush, thus giving me a moment to compose myself once more. I must not appear weak, but must rise to this wonderful challenge I have been offered, even if it is just for the short period of Her Ladyship's stay at the Hall. With renewed energy I turn around and smile confidently.

"Will that be all, M'Lady?"

I really don't know what I'm supposed to do bar being at her beck and call, yet there is no respite for me as she leans forward on the edge of the bed and tightly grasps both of my hands. I feel very unsure about the whole situation and her odd behaviour, especially when it is followed by a rather childlike chant.

"Warm hands, warm heart! That's what Mama used to say, warm hands, warm heart, and you shall be my warm heart! I chose you because of those warm hands and they will heal me! Stay with me, Florenza! I cannot bear to be left on my own!"

I am reluctant to pull my hands away from her firm grip as I sense they give her some comfort and vow to myself to make her stay as pleasant as I can to calm her down. Thus, the new pattern of my life is settled, for I know this will be a huge challenge and I must rise to the occasion by trying to understand the eccentric behaviour of Lady Louisa.

When I was about seven years old, I recall one erratic stormy day in late spring when we had been deluged with giant hailstones, followed by violent thunderstorms and then a severe wind that whirled and veered, threatening the young shoots in our fields. Henry, Tom and Pa had battled against it securing what they could or moving the likes of stray tools and cans into the safety of the privy. The winds had grown wilder throughout the day forming themselves into a frightening whirlwind that tore through our village, ripping saplings from the ground and even shifting some of the thatch upon our roof. Well, my life suddenly feels as if I have been drawn into that whirlwind and thrust out into another world, as the changes come swift and fast.

No longer do I share an attic room with Emma, but am allocated a small side room near to Her Ladyship's rooms. It feels more like an enlarged cupboard, but my heart melted when I saw the little bed, with its flowery top cover and even my little carved owl sitting proud alongside a china dish Ma had pressed me to take as a reminder of home. My few possessions had miraculously been transferred, including fresh dark uniforms I had now to wear. They felt so soft to my touch I was suddenly overwhelmed by the changes that had happened without my knowledge and the speed with which it had been executed.

Had this all be prearranged by His Lordship? Why was I selected when clearly other servants were better placed to take on this temporary role? Or were they forewarned that a mad woman was being brought here? Maybe I was deemed the fool who could take on that role as others feared the consequences. At first those questions abounded in my turbulent mind, but not for long. I sensed a growing element of excitement at the opportunities it might reveal and I was ready for to tackle them and prove myself worthy.

Chapter 20
Serving

In spite of my doubts, I feel quite proud that I have been designated to care for Lady Louisa. She doesn't ask a lot of me, but is more desperate for just companionship and conversation. After only a few days I began to try and assess her strange moods by the nature of her ramblings. Right now, I am engaged in a small sewing repair to one of the cuffs of her outdoor coat.

"He never came back, you know, just disappeared to the other side of the world. Do you have a beau, Gibbs?"

As she gazes out from her draped window I see the wistful look in her eyes, and sense the pain she is expressing of a lost friend and possible lover.

"No, M'Lady. My mama says men are always the cause of our troubles."

I not sure what made me say that and accidentally prick my finger as I darn, which I see as a timely warning to curb my tongue. I am further startled as the image of young Albert forms clearly in my mind. Life has been swiftly changed for me over recent months and I scarcely think about those I know back in High Weldon other than my own family. I'd already forgotten about that exciting day at the fair when Albert had been there to escort us and somehow it had felt good being in his presence. Yet I had not once given him a thought as my life had taken its twists and turns, taking me away from the simple village life I lived. There has been no further news of my sister Harriet, and I can only assume this will be causing my parents great anguish. My thoughts are abruptly interrupted by the next outburst as she turns to face me.

"You shall come back with me to London, Gibbs. In springtime the parks are alive with new blossoms, full of people glad to be out in the fresh air, riding their trusty steeds or enjoying a leisurely carriage ride."

She walks restlessly around her room, gazing from her window out over the parkland where the trees are bending as gusty March winds twist their boughs. I watch her with some suspicion, half believing the country myths I was brought up with about the madness of March affecting the human soul. Yet her words also serve to fill me with excited anticipation of what my future might be like. She then sits dejectedly in one of her pink chairs, sighing and rocking her head from side to side with an occasional muttered word or two.

I have already become familiar with her repeated actions that denote her anxieties as she starts to scratch her left wrist. It doesn't take long before a large inflamed red patch appears. I put down my work and head for one of the small drawers in her bedside cabinet, retrieving a jar of a soothing balm, which I bring over to her. She sits passively, content for me to gently apply the cream on the reddened areas and it pleases me to see a hint of a smile curl on her lips, but that calmness is soon gone as her next outburst shatters the serenity I had hoped to achieve.

"I hate it here, Gibbs, simply hate it! It's so abysmally dull in the country. The silence makes me have one of my bad heads. Oh, I do miss the buzz of city life, the street noises and conversations and invitations."

As the last words are wistfully spoken she closes her eyes and I am fully aware of the silence in the room that she has come to hate. I so want to sit and talk with her, offer her comforting advice as I would if one of my sisters were troubled. I even visualise us walking out together or taking a carriage ride out in the grounds, until my reverie is broken by her soft moaning as she cradles her aching head in two hands. I immediately push those thoughts aside, seeing her distress.

"Shall I get you something to help the pain, M'Lady?"

"Oh, my dear girl, the little flower Florenza, what would I do without you? Could you send for a soothing powder and some hot milk? Then I will take my rest."

With a polite nod I leave the room, gently closing the door before heading along the blue corridor.

All is quiet and I stand for a moment to compose myself. Who am I? It feels like one big confusion in my head. To my family I will be forever Flo, yet I now steel myself to answer to Gibbs, or the stupid Florenza, when all I really crave is to be Florence once more—Miss Florence. For one brief moment the image of Reverend Henderson forms in my mind, and I am struck by the effect it has on me, for a calmness fills me and I feel truly thankful as if he himself had actually been there endorsing my final thoughts.

Taking a deep breath, I hesitate once more and find myself gazing at one of the delicate Chinese vases. I know I shouldn't, but I can't resist a gentle touch to admire its beauty. What I'd imagined to be a flowery pattern I now see as a watery landscape with small figures dotted around, with such delicate painted faces that I marvel at the workmanship. What I'm really doing is delaying the moment I enter the kitchens for since my new appointment to serve, albeit a temporary one, I have encountered a mild hostility from some of the staff. Mrs Baynton can hardly bring herself to look straight at me, let alone address me by name. Maisie is the only one who can still cheerfully smile at me if I go in with any specific meal requests, and today I am so relieved to see just her and Emma working alone at the tables.

"Oh Flo, oh dear! Beg pardon, but we've been told to call you Miss now and we do miss you!"

Emma giggles at the little word pun and I can't help but grin too. It feels so odd with all these various names I am called by from the varying members of the household, but it pleases me to hear her warm and friendly words.

"I miss your happy faces, too. Just wondering where Mrs Baynton is."

Maisie is nodding towards the door that leads to the housekeeper's rooms.

"She said she had some special job to arrange and quite honestly it's been a blessing just having the kitchen to ourselves for the afternoon. What is it you'll be wanting for Her Ladyship, then? We've both been wondering how you are coping with her, her being a bit mad, like."

I know they are probing for information or titbits of gossip that I might disclose, but it will be in vain. My lips stay sealed.

"She's asked for a hot milk now, then her usual tray tonight, as she prefers to eat in her rooms. Thank you, Maisie, and now I have a further errand to see to."

Leaving them to their work I brace myself for the next encounter, which thankfully passes with a minimum of words, as I am reluctantly handed the special sachet of powder. Mrs Baynton has to retrieve it from a securely locked medicine cabinet within her quarters. She does not address me directly, but looks with some disdain upon the paper sachet now in my hand before adding in her aloof voice, "Much good that'll do her!"

It is with some relief I hasten back up the spiral stairs to deliver the package as speedily as I can. A maid is leaving Her Ladyship's room and nods politely to me.

"The hot milk as you requested, Miss. I left it just inside the door so as not to disturb the lady."

It is somewhat of a mystery to me what these little packets contain, but they seem invaluable to calm Lady Louisa and to help her sleep soundly. Whisked in with milk seems to make it more acceptable than with water, although I often note how she grimaces on taking the first sip. Seeing her drift so rapidly into a deep sleep, her body limp upon the sumptuous bed, I feel a little envious and one irrational part of my mind craves to know what that feels like, to be so oblivious to the outside world, free of any worries and responsibilities. As she sleeps I feel a wonderful freedom, just tidying a few garments into the closet, feeling the soft strings of pearls that she tends to leave casually in a pink cut glass dish upon the dressing table. Their lustre fascinates me and I think of Ma, and how perhaps one day I shall be able to afford to treat her to something similar.

Chapter 21
April

Spring has come with a sudden rush, a welcome blossoming of the trees around the parkland and a feeling of gentle warmth in the air. It serves to make my spirits rise when I am tasked with escorting Lady Louisa as she takes a morning stroll around the courtyard. I no longer serve His Lordship or see many of the other staff unless we pass by in the corridors. However, only last week I was informed that Lord Gressingham wished to speak to me and was summoned to the Golden Room. I still feel a little in awe when I am in his presence and tend to brace myself for the worst. I was admitted by Withers without so much as a snide comment and entered the room to see Lord Gressingham gazing out of the big bay window. Turning to face me, I could sense something was on his mind, for his eyebrows were furrowed as if in deep thought.

"Thank you coming, Florence. A rather delicate matter, but where to begin?"

He had paused after those few words, and I stood there waiting for a possible reprimand, but his next words startled me even more.

"Please take a seat, for I feel you should be put in the picture."

I had hesitated until he pointed to a nearby chair and I sat there with a strange feeling of confusion and vulnerability. Even my customary smile evaded me, although I was truly thankful for the soft way he spoke to me as he continued.

"My sister has spoken highly of you, Florence, and I am grateful you have been so patient with her."

He paused and stroked his whiskery beard, head down as if searching for the right words.

"But you must understand she has always suffered from bouts of madness and she could turn on you and harm you. Now, has that ever happened?"

It felt alarming to hear such a blunt statement, as apart from Lady Louisa's little outbursts and occasional headaches, she has shown me only kindness and consideration. Too stunned to answer, I simply shook my head from side to side. What he had then added set my pulse racing and my head spinning.

"I had hoped that time spent here would have calmed her more, but I fear her London physicians have been correct all along and that she will have to be admitted to a secure place for proper treatment. I shall be organising her return next week. Until then, I must ask you to be ever vigilant and stay close by her. She will probably insist you accompany her, but that will be your choice, Florence."

It was a lot to try and understand. In my naivety I had not appreciated the severity of Her Ladyship's malady, still thinking that some love and understanding would be the best medicine for her. I had watched as Lord Gressingham looked up at one of the family portraits hanging on the wall, a wistful gaze that masked sadness and left me with many confused thoughts. As the ensuing silence continued it appeared to signal an end to the interview so I rose from the chair, curtseyed and took my leave.

"Thank you, M'Lord."

There was much to toss over in my mind with this startling news, for it seemed to herald yet another short-lived phase in my life. I stood motionless outside the large door, trying to take it all in. I still clung to the fact that I could be asked to stay with Her Ladyship and escort her back to her London home. I even imagined I could be with her on visits to art galleries, or even the theatre houses I'd heard of, but those were fanciful thoughts as I realised it would soon come to a swift end if His Lordship's orders were to be carried out. I had returned to blue wing with a heavy heart, vowing to make the most of these last precious days in her company.

Today we are taking the air in the rose garden, and among the budding bushes we behold a wonderful sight with all the spring bulbs planted in the borders. Lady Louisa seems a little wistful as her fingers stoke the bright petals in passing.

"Such a pity that daffodils have no scent. Oh look, Gibbs! A clump of hyacinths just beside the wall. Now they will surely smell sweet!"

Leaving my side, she has run down the path and fallen to her knees. At first, I think she has tripped but then I realise she is leaning over the flower heads in order to smell them.

"Oh, so beautiful. Do come down with me, my precious Florenza!"

One hand is outstretched, inviting me to join her, so I willingly comply and lower myself to my knees alongside her. If this is what is required to keep her happy and contented, I will do anything. The rich perfume fills my nostrils and warms my spirits and puts all thoughts of the future out of my head. With our heads so close together she turns and faces me, looking deep into my eyes.

"Come home with me, dear child. You and I will escape this horrid place and be free to enjoy our city life!"

I can see these thoughts have invigorated her as she jumps up, and commences to spin in circles, her dress flaring and catching on the prickly rose bushes, and for just that second I can sense this might be part of her madness. I hasten to grab her and hold her fast, and as I do so, she begins to scream for help.

"Simpson! Help me! They have come to put me away! Help! She's hurting me!"

These cries are so loud that a couple of gardeners have rushed to see what is happening and I'm rather thankful they wrench Lady Louisa from my grasp and half carry her into the courtyard. The cries have also alerted Lord Gressingham, who runs down the steps with several strong servants. I am trailing behind feeling helpless in this current situation yet the reality of what I'd previously been told begins to sink in. I attempt to follow as the raving lady is taken indoors, but am held back by Withers as he gives directions to the staff. Only now do I realise I am shaking with the shock of the past few minutes. His Lordship walks over and indicates with his hand to approach him.

"My sister will be cared for and perhaps it is best if you leave her to rest."

I nod, feeling ashamed that I had failed in my duties. He does not comment but his eyes seem to scan me up and down.

"You've had a shock Florence, but please do not blame yourself. I think it best you retire to your room and we'll get cook to send up a restorative drink and food."

He stretches out one hand as if to comfort me, but it falls to his side and he turns to go in. I am left standing there on the bottom step, glad of the rails to support my still trembling body and lost in thought.

"Are you all right, Miss? Here, let me help you up the steps."

I recognise the voice from an earlier encounter as the maid Jane, the one who looked much older and more confident than I had felt when we were being inspected. Right now, I am just thankful to feel her arm gently supporting mine as we pass through the grand entrance hall and for the kindness she shows me. I do feel very weak and am fearful of falling as I walk along the corridors. There is a small parlour next to the kitchens and I am forced into a chair and plied with a hot drink that I detect has something stronger added to it. It serves its purpose and I begin to feel steadier and my breathing less laboured.

"Mrs Baynton asked if I would sit with you as it has been such a shock for you. Apparently when Her Ladyship came last year, she even hit out at the girl who looked after her, cut her across the face, so naturally Mrs B was concerned a similar thing might happen to you. Did she hit you today?"

97

"I'm finding it just so hard understand. No, she was behaving quite normally I thought, until…"

I search in vain for the trigger that so altered her behaviour, left wondering if the beautiful scents were to blame.

"I think you've been very brave and I have to confess I was once envious that you were chosen instead of me. In truth, I don't think I could have coped at all, whereas you've been great company for Her Ladyship. I've heard tell that you did your very best and His Lordship is really grateful."

I can feel tears welling behind my eyes and reach in my pocket for a handkerchief. I feign blowing my nose so as to surreptitiously wipe them away and not allow myself to appear weak. I look up at her and smile.

"Thank you so much for helping me. I'll be fine now. Thank you again."

Jane touches my hand, squeezing it gently in a reassuring way.

"You did your best and that's what counts."

Left to my own device, I go over the afternoon's events, fearing that this second opportunity of bettering myself will now come to an abrupt end. I have to force down half a sandwich to mask the strong taste of the drink, but I have little appetite for anything, just a desire to sleep and blot out the reality of the situation.

Chapter 22
Opportunities

Over the next few days I had to come to terms with the traumatic events of that garden episode, and it all proved quite a challenge for me. Mrs Baynton had asked me to join her in her private rooms the very next day, although it was not a request I had relished. I was invited to sit upon a low ottoman seat whilst she addressed me. However, her tone was one of sympathy and understanding as she explained that I would be excused duties, as Her Ladyship would be cared for by those who know what is best for her. She will be attended by Miss Jones who arrives today. By that I conclude she means someone with nursing experience or perhaps a person to guard against any further outbursts, but it leaves me feeling worthless as if I had been unfairly used, with only the good memories of our times together that I had so enjoyed.

"Lord Gressingham has told me to tell you that he is more than grateful for how you have coped and is shocked that you were subjected to one of Her Ladyship's outbursts. He is still hoping that you will consider accompanying Her Ladyship on her return journey. That will be your choice, Florence."

Was I hearing correctly? It came as a bit of a shock to hear her call me that name, unlike those January days when I was made to feel humble in my kitchen role.

I had watched the housekeeper carefully, as she leant over the table to address me. I sensed she was almost pleading with me to answer and yet I hesitated, unsure of the right decision.

"He certainly hopes you will agree to his request and assures me that you would still retain some position within his household upon your return."

Then to my surprise, she added, "Should you agree, it has been decided by His Lordship that you may spend three days at your home with your family and return next Tuesday to be ready to travel to London the next day. However, if you do not wish to proceed…"

I realised that Mrs Baynton had deliberately paused to offer that enticement, and I took no hesitation in replying, "Thank you, Mrs Baynton. I will escort Lady Louisa on her return and am truly grateful for His Lordship's kindness."

I felt I ought to express my thanks to her too, but found that harder to do. As I rose to leave the room I simply added, "I appreciate your understanding."

It was all I felt I could say but I did half smile at her. With the interview concluded her face had hardened once more and her words become curt and precise.

"There will be a cart for you by the stables at two this afternoon. You can take that."

Thus, my immediate short-term future was mapped out, but the one compelling thing that was uppermost in my heart was the rare chance I was being given to visit our capital city. I had seen illustrations in old newspapers of many famous buildings with their grand façades, the Houses of Parliament and St Paul's cathedral but I never dreamt that such an opportunity would ever be available to me to actually travel there. As the little cart jogs along the driveway away from the Hall, I am like a genie released from a bottle, free from any pressures, left to wonder what treats will be in store. Somehow all thoughts of the problems I might face returning with a slightly mad lady were pushed firmly out of mind. Now I'm just excited that I'm on my way back home.

The clattering of hooves outside our cottage has alerted Ma. Her curiosity makes her appear from the side, wiping her hands on the long work apron, no doubt expecting it to be a delivery of food. It is so wonderful to see her and she clearly looks startled to see me stepping down from the cart.

"Oh Flo! My darling girl, this is a wonderful surprise!"

Ma looks tired, with dark rings around her eyes and I can see the doubts she may be having as to my sudden appearance in the working week.

"Oh Ma, it is so good to see you!"

I try hard not to let my emotions get the better of me, even though there is a lump in my throat as Ma hugs me warmly.

"Come in! Come in!"

I feel like a small, secure child again as with arms linked Ma leads me around to the entrance, and I see again the familiar garden with its plum tree in bud, not quite ready to burst forth with its customary white blossom.

I am truly thankful Ma doesn't rush me for explanations, but we sit at our long kitchen table and I savour a slice of her famous fruit cake with my own cherished mug of tea. I feel the little chip on its rim and it is so reassuring to be home with familiar things around me.

Ma alone will be privy to the events of the past few days, and I feel I can tell her everything whilst we work together preparing a meal for our family. It is easier to speak whilst I work, but I find myself making light of the events and omitting the garish details about Her Ladyship by simply suggesting she had some health issues. Ma listens thoughtfully and does not interrupt until I have finished.

"But we thought you was in the kitchens and now you're a telling me you've been asked to be a servant to one of them toffs! Oh, our Flo! Wait 'til the others come in and hear that. They'll be as proud as I am to hear that great news!"

There's a part of me that wants to keep it my own special secret and I bargain with Ma to go along with a simpler version of the story, that I am to go to London along with some of the household to His Lordship's town property. I beg her not to mention the real reasons I have been summoned. She does so with a certain sadness, as I could see she was desperate to boast of my better position within service.

It is heart-warming to see my family once more, to revel in their banter as we sit squashed around the table, the air buzzing

101

with their lively jokes and quips and snippets of what had been happening in the village.

"You missed a laugh three days ago, Flo, when poor old John Groom got so drunk he fell in the road and landed right in a cow splat! Phew! He ponged for days afterwards!"

Jack has shot up over the past few months, quite the young man with a hint of furry lip hair, but he is still the one to make us chuckle. Tom has yet to recognise me, even though Ma had repeatedly reminded him that I was Flo, his sister. He is still staring blankly at me, and I begin to wonder if I've changed that much. Pa is at the head of the table, and I note how much frailer he has become, seeing his hands shaking as he messily spoons his rabbit stew and noting how he refrains from speaking out bluntly in his accustomed manner. Lizzie looks well, has filled out and seems far more confident as she chats about how she now is trusted to serve in Graves" grocery store, and how the nice Miss Millicent who had taken over shop treats her kindly.

"I can even use the new meat slicer now and it cuts a real treat! Ma knows, don't you, because I'm allowed to bring home the cuts from the end piece!"

Ma is nodding her approval, but laughter erupts once more as Joe sings out, "Yum yum, pig's bum! You can't have some!"

Ma lovingly clouts him round the head with the back of her hand, chiding him for his rudeness and I half expect Pa to add his stern remarks, too. But he still sits as if in a dream, so when he does speak it comes as a bit of a shock.

"So, our Flo, you home for good now? Got yourself fired, have you? That's just typical of them there nobs up at the Hall; look down on us lot as if we were muck."

Silence falls as he continues eating.

"Whisht, Father. Flo has just come to see us to say she'll be working a short while for His Lordship, but up at his London home instead. She just wanted to see us before she went."

I breathe an inner sigh that Ma has stuck to our story and it appears to satisfy everyone's curiosity.

As the meal ends and Lizzie helps Ma to clear plates away, my eldest brother Henry suddenly appears, sticking his tousled head around the door, and stands there grinning at us all, his swarthy face all aglow from working out in the woods.

"Any food left for a hard-working slave, Ma?"

"Oh lad, you'll be the death of me, making me jump like that! Get yourself inside and I'll rustle up something for you. Look who's joined us tonight!"

Ma is pointing towards me, but she is equally delighted that another of her brood has turned up, but it makes it even more poignant that two sisters are missing and not one word has been said as to their whereabouts.

As Henry munches, we remain huddled around the table and I get to hear how my other siblings are faring. Mary can't wait to show me her newly acquired scrapbook and all the cuttings from newspapers.

"Miss Cross lets me have all her old copies, and look, Flo! I've got ones all about London places, see? This one's of the streets and they've got funny sorts of carriages that are pulled on tracks. Miss Cross says they are called horse-drawn buses. You have to climb up some stairs to get to the top and I think that looks very scary!"

I look through the pages of curled cuttings where the flour paste Ma would have given her hadn't quite stuck everything down. There were the images of famous landmarks we'd heard of in stories and of which I might soon get to see. I am thankful to see she has also got a page devoted to advertisements, in particular of the latest kitchen utensils, so remark on that instead.

"Well, you have been a busy bee, our Mary!"

"I've decided I shall be a cook, just like you and make Ma just as proud of me!"

As she stands next to me, I give her a well-deserved hug, then summon the courage to quietly ask Lizzie about my other two sisters. Apparently, it is quite common for our Sue to sleep over at the farm where she works, but then I ask about Harriet.

Lizzie puts a finger to her lips and I sense she doesn't want to upset her mother.

"She ran off with Reggie Mason and now Ma won't have her talked about."

And so I learn how this scoundrel claimed he was going to marry her when she becomes of age. They had heard about his grand plans to run a public house in the nearby town where Harriet would be a barmaid instead of working at the local factory. It all sounds very dubious to me and doesn't allay my fears for her wellbeing. So now I aim to enjoy these precious family times by engaging my big brother in a light-hearted way, desperate to hear the latest news about his latest sweetheart.

"Now Master Henry, what's this I hear about the lovely Miss Ivy?"

Chapter 23
Travel

The time came for me to bid farewell to my family and I arrived back at the Hall as planned. Here I was informed of the arrangements put in place for Lady Louisa and myself to travel together. His Lordship would also be coming up to his London home. I felt extremely nervous of how she would behave towards me, but what disturbed me was hearing that I was barred from attending Her Ladyship until the day when we were to travel, merely given other general duties to fill my time. Apparently she is being given professional help and I am not needed. So yet again I am left wondering why I have been drawn into this unusual situation.

Wednesday morning dawns after a restless night's sleep. I almost feel like running away from everything. I am called to her rooms with instructions to pack her effects for our journey and I feel quite nervous. The door is opened by a stern-faced lady who speaks to me in soft tones.

"Do not hesitate to ring the bell if M'Lady has a strange turn. I will only be in the next room."

I'm put on my guard, fearing in what state I will find her. However, I need not have feared, for when I do enter her room I find her very calm, as if nothing untoward has ever occurred. She holds out her hands in a pleading way and grasps mine as I stand there, as if we are reconciling after the previous altercation in the gardens.

"Florence, my dear Florenza! I thought you had abandoned me. But you're here and you must never leave my side! Promise me!"

Although I have now been made aware of her unpredictable moods, I still feel it best to pull away and not get too involved.

"I'm here to pack your clothes for our little journey, M'Lady, and I'll be going with you, so you don't have to fret about that any more. Now, your trunk has already been brought up, so are you happy for me to start?"

My smile is not only for her, but also masks my excitement at this golden opportunity I have been given. I do not yet want to contemplate how things will be if His Lordship's plans proceed to have her put away or what my future might be after that. I busily apply myself to see her effects are carefully stowed and then spend my last night in the seclusion of my little box room.

I wake with excitement, knowing today we are going. I still have orders not to go to Her Ladyship's rooms, but to assemble in the courtyard at ten o'clock. There is a great bustle of activity as trunks are packed and the coachman waits patiently soothing the restless horses. Withers takes me to one side as we prepare to travel and it unsettles me.

"Just to warn you, Gibbs, Lord Gressingham has arranged for his sister and yourself to be escorted by Jones. She is the qualified nurse who has been attending her while you were visiting your family, and she will be on hand should there be any disruption en route. His Lordship will also be travelling with you in his carriage and will meet you at the station."

He has spoken to me in such a stern way that it only adds to my confusion. I begin to think it was actually me they want gone from the household as even Mrs Baynton is standing in the courtyard to watch us boarding the coach. She does not speak, but looks relieved as Lady Louisa mounts the steps accompanied by the austere lady dressed all in black. She has silently taken her place alongside Her Ladyship in the carriage. Just as I am about to follow, I hear the words behind me:

"No doubt you'll be back here sooner than you think!"

I choose to ignore those remarks, yet silently have to acknowledge there is a certain truth in what she has said. I am directed by Withers to sit on the opposite seat as the door is firmly shut. This flusters me for fear I will be constantly looking at their faces. One appears so stern while Lady Louisa is looking slightly flustered as the warm May sunshine magnifies the heat in the confined space. But she remains quiet and still throughout that short journey and I suspect she may have been given sedatives to calm her down.

Instead, I gaze out of the carriage window seeing trees flash by and unknown buildings as we make our way through Felborough towards the station. There is little conversation during that short ride apart from some comments about the blossom on the trees, but I give a reassuring smile once or twice to Lady Louisa, when I can see that Miss Jones is gazing the other way.

His Lordship's carriage is already drawn up outside the imposing station entrance and he directs our select party towards a grand tiled room within the station where they can wait in comfort. I am detailed to carry a personal portmanteau for Her Ladyship as she is firmly ushered in by her chaperone. I could hardly believe how warm it feels inside, lit by a crackling fire, but after they have been seated I think it best to wait outside along with some of Lord Gressingham's personal staff. It shakes me to note that Withers is also there, yet I should have realised he would come along to assist His Lordship. I watch him striding down the long platform and conversing with a porter who is struggling with a laden trolley of trunks and crates that await the incoming train. Even now I feel I have to pinch myself to believe that I shall be riding in a railway carriage. When the belching engine draws near to the station I can feel my heart racing, imagining it is heading straight for me. The noise is so great I well understand why my brother Henry had once spoken of them as "fiery dragons".

It is with some relief when the tedious journey nears its end. I feel completely out of my depth with the strangeness of it all.

It all passes in a nervous blur as I take in the rows of tall buildings that loom high on both sides of the London streets. We have to take a hired Hackney cab from the station and as it jolts along, we are jerked forward when the horses are reigned in to avoid any collision with other carriages trying to cross the road. Lady Louisa is becoming more agitated by the minute so I am greatly relieved when we draw up outside the elegant house. Miss Jones is swift to dismount and can be seen beckoning with her right hand. Withers quickly appears and together, their hands gripping firmly on her upper arms, they escort Lady Louisa towards the house where a servant in smart livery has been alerted to the noise. The large front door is now swung wide to allow their entry. Lord Gressingham has alighted from a cab now, drawn up behind ours, and he strides over to join them indoors. I find myself waiting despondently and unsure of what to do until the servant reappears.

"I will take this for Lady Louisa."

He seizes the portmanteau from my reluctant grasp and leaves me feeling very vulnerable without the security it has offered me through the journey.

"This is the way. Follow me. Lord Gressingham has asked you to wait for him in the parlour. I will show you where that is."

I am led through into a room that takes my breath away, for this is even grander than the rooms at Branswick Hall. There are two long windows that seem to stretch from ceiling to floor that are framed with deep red velvet curtains. Several small, ornately carved chairs are casually placed around, some near a highly polished table. I am soothed by the regular beat from a huge clock upon the mantelpiece and equally enchanted by an elaborate oil lamp that stands upon another table. It has such a delicate glass shade and all I can think of is how much this would amaze Ma. My eyes are wondering at the lush thick quality of the carpet when Lord Gressingham enters the room, looking rather flustered. He is mopping his brow with a large handkerchief and then sits heavily upon one of the chairs. I can feel my heart rate begin to rise, but I use all my willpower to appear calm and composed. He takes his time before addressing me.

"A sorry business indeed, but we've finally made it here and I want to thank you for agreeing to accompany my sister. I gather from Miss Jones that you helped to keep her calm during the tedious journey and for that I'm very grateful."

I can't claim to have done anything that would have kept Her Ladyship calm as I am still convinced she had been given a sleeping draught, so maybe it was just the sight of a familiar face for her to relate to.

"Miss Jones is an experienced nurse and as such will be taking control of her needs."

I brace myself for what is about to come as I foresee a swift return back to the country house. I am rather stunned to hear him add,

"Please take a seat, as I need to make your position clear."

I'm in such a dazed state I do as he commands and await his verdict.

"In the absence of Mrs Baynton, who would normally give your orders, the housekeeper here is unaware of this current situation regarding my sister's health. I would like to keep it that way. I have been forced to arrange her removal to a secure place where she will receive professional treatment, but it must be done with the utmost secrecy. It will take place within the next few days."

Just hearing that saddens me and I find it rather odd. Perhaps this has to be done to avoid any public disgrace.

"Now, I want you to understand that this will involve your continued cooperation in maintaining a stable daily routine. We are most fortunate to have secured the services of Miss Jones who will be in charge. However, she will call on you to spend a short time each day so as to keep my sister calm during her brief stay in London. I have to insist you say nothing about her condition that would cause alarm amongst the current staff employed here. Now is that clear?"

It baffles me to think about these demands and the weird fact that his London household staff are not to be informed. From my past experiences I know that it is all too easy for staff to gossip about the goings on of the gentry. Keeping them ignorant of Her Ladyship's mad spells will be an almost impossible task.

I feel bold enough to challenge His Lordship, but agitated at the same time. "Thank you for explaining M'Lord. I can only do my best, but is there no other way Lady Louisa can be treated?"

I watch as he drops his head into his outstretched hands, shaking it from side to side whilst muttering, "Sadly not, I'm afraid. I shall see you are personally rewarded for your service."

He makes his way out looking very dejected and I am left standing in a vacuum.

Chapter 24
Upper Brook Street

The London home where Lord Gressingham resides is in Upper Brook Street just a short way from leafy Grosvenor Square. The white stonework glistens in the afternoon sunshine and contrasts with the black balcony rails at the upper level. Here the spring bulbs are putting on a vivid show with their pink and red flower heads as they sit amongst the greenery in large troughs that are attached to the rails. The front step, freshly scrubbed each morning, shines with its marble tiles and complements the imposing façade, but I do not notice any other details for now I feel like a lost sheep out in the fields, having been left in this awe-inspiring room, so it is pleasing when a friendly face appears from behind the door and a plump middle-aged woman wearing a dark grey dress approaches to greet me.

"You're very welcome, Miss, and His Lordship has asked me to see you settled in your room. I'm Mrs Blake, the best cook in the street, and you won't want for ought while you're here with us! Now, normally you would be seen by our resident housekeeper, Miss Grant, but she and most of the permanent staff are off abroad with the Countess for six months. I suppose you know this house is used by her friends and it's such a pleasure to welcome Lord Gressingham back to stay. Oh, hark at me going on! And I'm a guessing you're in need of the facilities right now after your journey, so follow me!"

This is the oddest piece of information I have been given, knowing that this beautiful house does in fact belong to someone else. The mention of a Countess is also confusing, as in all the time I've worked at Branswick Hall there has never been any mention of Lady Gressingham, so maybe she is the mysterious countess I'm hearing about. I hurry to follow the bustling lady up the stairs to the first floor where I am led into a small bedroom.

"I had my orders to put you in this room as it will be easier for you to attend Lady Louisa."

She is pointing to a door in the wall which I can only assume connects to another room.

"Now I'll leave you to make yourself comfy. The closet is just to your left. I've been asked to get an early meal for all you weary travellers and I'm told that Withers will show you where we eat, then guide you around the house so you become familiar with the rooms."

Left alone I have a rare moment to relax, but my curiosity impels me to explore the room. There is more in it than I could have ever dream of. One single bed lies adjacent to the wall and I can't resist feeling its soft, padded covering. It is framed by an ornate metal headboard against which are two pure white pillows that shimmer in the late afternoon rays of the sun. A small, polished writing table and chair are placed alongside the opposite side and I can see a further stand bearing the porcelain wash bowl and water jug in readiness for me. I can't quite believe my good fortune, but now there is a desperate urgency for me to seek the closet and relieve myself. Afterwards I feel refreshed as I splash my face with the cold water, relishing that little luxury as I wipe away the traces of the train journey.

My well-worn suitcase has already been delivered to the room and I make short work of unpacking the few clothes I have. Curious to look around, I am surprised to find two new working outfits already hanging in corner cupboard. They are far superior to my present dark grey skirt, so I make the bold decision to change. To my amazement the dress fits perfectly, with its sleek cut so unlike the style of dress I have worn before. There is a small hand mirror upon a little shelf and now I can't resist picking it up and taking a long look at myself. Just that one action causes my heart to skip a beat, for I barely recognise the image reflected back.

"Oh Albert, if you could only see me now!"

Such unexpected thoughts startle me and quickly dispel any feelings of grandeur that I may have had. Now I must brace myself to face this new challenge, however brief.

It seems strange with so few staff working here at present apart from the boy at the door and a kitchen maid, so it was pleasant to talk with Mrs Blake and feel at ease as I enjoyed a wonderful roast dinner. I was not to be called for on that first evening so was keen to retire to my bedroom. Maybe my eyes were looking heavy but it pleased me to hear her say:

"Best you have an early night and then you'll be refreshed for Her Ladyship tomorrow."

Although I was extremely tired from travelling, I slept fitfully, waking to strange noises and smells, so that by this morning I could not face eating any breakfast in spite of being coaxed by the kind Mrs Blake, who tempted me with a dish of scrambled eggs. My head is all of a dither with the many uncertainties of my position.

Last week's events have become a confused blur and now I find myself standing by this grand bay window, draped in the finest of muslins, waiting to be called into Her Ladyship's rooms. Outside there is constant activity as delivery carts rattle by and upright gentlemen in tall top hats stride purposely along Upper Brook Street with their canes. I realise I should feel privileged to be living in such a grand house when so little is being asked of me, but that brings a guilt of its own. Lord Gressingham was most insistent I spend a short time each day with his sister but far from seeing to her needs, I have been instructed to amuse her, talk with her or read as she so desires. It is all rather puzzling. The sound of a door opening brings me back to the present moment as the nurse hovers there, midway between the two connected rooms.

"You are to come now and sit with Her Ladyship, read to her, but on no account must you leave her side. Is that understood?"

It doesn't seem to merit an answer, so I simply hasten across the room, squeeze past her stiffened body as she maintains guard until I am through. It is with some relief I hear the click of the door lock and know that I am alone with M'Lady. Today she is lying on a low sort of day bed all clothed in white. My initial thoughts are that she is still wearing her night gown, but then I see the delicate lace drapes that hang from each shoulder and the glimmer from tiny seed pearls that adorn the bodice of her dress. She looks pale, almost bride-like, yet appears uninterested with her eyes fixed firmly towards a gilded clock above the fireplace. She does not speak today, just ignores me whilst fanning herself in an attempt to keep cool. I think hard how best to communicate with her so decide upon a cheerful approach.

"It's such a lovely warm day, M'Lady, perhaps a little fresh air to cool you down?"

Forgetting that I am meant to stay by her side I step towards the window, but her sharp retort unsettles me.

"You can't do that! They've locked them tight. Fools! They think I might try and climb out and escape. They think I'm mad you know! But you don't think that, do you?"

Her sad face pleads as I struggle in vain to loosen the window catch and it is all the more alarming to see the precautions that are taken to confine the poor lady.

"Come and sit with me, Simpson. Tell me about the parades again!"

I brace myself, take a seat alongside then remind her that I am not Simpson.

"I'm Gibbs, M'Lady. I served you when you stayed at Branswick Hall."

Lady Louisa lets her head fall backwards and scans the ceiling as if searching for her memories. The scalloped fan falls

114

to the floor and I retrieve it, savouring the feel of the French lace and coolness of its ivory stems.

"Gibbs, you say? No, no, you came to tea, I do remember. Of course, you are my dear friend Florenza! How did you know I was back in London?"

This is the most distressing conversation that has taken place during the times I've been with her and it chokes me to see her so confused. All my previous aspirations to prove she was perfectly sane are speedily evaporating and my attempts to establish some continuity are proving futile. There seems to be little point in trying to reason with her, so I decide to bolster her spirits and chat about all the lovely things that happen in the summertime.

"All the spring blossoms are out on the trees, M'Lady, and soon you'll be able to ride through the parks and see them!"

The very thought sees her eyes light up as she replies, "You will come with me, won't you? And we shall smell the perfumed air and wear our best finery to impress!"

I am lost for words and sense the futility of it all. "Shall I continue reading, M'Lady? Now, where did we get to?"

I pick up the slim novel and commence reading to her.

Chapter 25
Departure

A single rap upon my door wakes me in the morning and I hear a soft voice that almost sings as it moves down the corridor.

"Wake-up call! Good morning!"

This is my third day and it still seems surreal to be here. I have no timepiece of my own, but know that in normal circumstances I would be bidden to rise early. Yet there is no pressure for me to do that and it still feels strange not to have those set routines.

I allow myself a few seconds before stirring, thinking back to yesterday and remembering the unusually happy afternoon I had spent with Lady Louisa. For once she displayed none of her bizarre behaviour like the day before, but had chatted to me as if we were the oldest of friends. It had given me a warm feeling of importance and belonging, one I liked very much and I don't want it to end.

I'm still getting used to the sounds of city life, the clatter of hooves, and people raucously shouting in their strange way out in the streets. Sometimes I'm already awake after hearing flocks of unruly starlings who regularly appear and congregate somewhere up on the rooftop. They chatter incessantly until startled by the frequent deliveries that are made as crates thud to the ground, often causing the birds to take flight. Today it's a pleasure to stretch my arms as I rise, feeling safe and secure in this pleasant bedroom, although I can hear slightly raised voices from below and it spurs me into action.

I am temporarily blinded by a shaft of light as I pull back the curtains revealing a blue sky. Then the fluttering green leaves from a nearby plane tree come into focus and I watch the bustling activity down at the rear of the house. Oh how different this all is from the restricted view of our cottage window back home, where you can just about see the vegetable beds and privy in the distance. I do not wish to think about such things right now, so wash and dress myself in readiness for what the day might bring.

I find Mrs Blake sitting by herself at the servant's dining table, sipping a mug of tea and peering with strained eyes at a worn newspaper as if trying to decipher the small print. There are no signs of any of the other staff, which does intrigue me, merely an eerie silence in the room. She greets me with a friendly grin.

"Well, it's just me and thee, although I expect you have gathered that. Help yourself to some of that porridge, oh and one for me, and we can have a good old chinwag without any interruption!"

As I ladle breakfast I'm puzzled by her comments, so I feel I need to question her.

"I'm sorry I am late coming down, Mrs Blake, and I do hope it hasn't put you about? Has there been a problem for the staff to deal with?"

The kindly cook places the newspaper on the table, and sighs.

"It looks like I'll be the one who has to break the news to you, so bring the bowls over here and just you sit yourself comfy while I explain."

Now I start to wonder if Lady Louisa has had another funny turn or become violent, so between supping the hot cereal I await the latest news.

"The long and the short of it is that Lady Louisa has been taken off early this morning, poor lambkin. Now, we all knows that His Lordship did his best for her, but she needs to be put away for her own safety."

I am shocked to hear this, pushing my half-finished breakfast away as reality sinks in of what I've just heard.

117

"Did you not hear her shouting out? Oh, and she hit one of the serving maids real bad, even cut her face with her sharp nails as she was being taken out to the special carriage. We know what she's like from the number of times they have stayed here in the past; some say it all started when she was left standing at the church altar and the swine she was meant to be marrying failed to turn up. They reckon it turned her brain and she was never the same again. She used to have a personal maid who she met in Italy and then there was a lot of gossip about the two of them. She got rather close to her... do you know what I mean? Not something I like to think about."

Mrs Blake pauses after her long flow of words to take breath, but wears a distinct look of disapproval on her face. I am left reeling at all these disclosures, as it is the first time I've heard any details about her previous life and it intrigues me to know more, especially after that final comment.

"Honestly, I didn't know anything about Her Ladyship and I still am at a loss to know why I was put with her. You see, I thought I was picked just to assist her when she stayed at Branswick Hall, on account of her previous maid suddenly leaving, but it always struck me as being very odd, seeing as I was just working in the kitchens."

The cook leans towards me, and pats my hand as it rests on the table.

"We've all known about her funny turns, both staff and family. I've been serving in Lord Gressingham's house when she's been staying in England and can recall the times she would be calling out for this foreign girl. Such a mouthful of a name, let me see if I can remember it? Something like Fiordelizza or Fiordelenza, and she was a right little madam who thought she was in charge. The only good thing about her was she kept Lady Louisa calm and we all found out why!"

With her arms firmly crossed Mrs Blake sits shaking her head from side to side. Then in whispered tones she leans towards me. "They was caught out doing a bit more than the kissing and cuddling, and I'll say no more!"

118

Her revelation brings to mind stories I'd once heard from my sister Sue when she left school. My family had been delighted that she had secured a great position with a local spinster lady living by her own means at a comfy home in the town of Felborough. Sue had been taken on as a scullery maid for this Miss Brown, but she soon realised that wasn't the role she was intended for. Miss Brown would follow her around often standing far too close to her and would pat her gently on the arms. She had been encouraged to call her employer Roberta, but as these advances became more pressing, Sue had been forced to leave and is now far more content with her farm work.

"Oh gosh! Maybe that's why I got picked? Do you think she wanted me for her own fancy? I thought she was being harshly treated by her brother and that she just needed a bit of understanding and friendship. I did try my best and she was simply very kind to me."

I don't mention the garden incident for now it all starts to make sense.

"What happened to this foreign person? Did she get dismissed?"

It is slowly dawning on me that my own position will be soon be brought to an abrupt end and yet I want to hear more whilst I have this rare opportunity talking to Mrs Blake.

"Oh yes. They said His Lordship threw her out and her belongings, and that's when his sister really started her wild behaviour. Kept calling out 'Florenza! Florenza!' 'cos that were her pet name for her. I expect it reminded her of the villa out in Florence where they would stay in the summer months."

Her words now remind me of something His Lordship said when he first spoke to me and talked of holidays in Italy. So that's why she had called me Florenza and I had imagined it was just teasing me about my own name. I listen avidly as the story unfolds.

"Such a rum do. Anyway, as I said, she's been taken off to one of them secure asylums and Lord Gressingham has upped and gone, too, along with his staff. I expect he'll be checking up on the work being done at his place over by Berkeley Square. I gather his wife is coming up from their other home in Sussex. That's a funny business, too! However, he gave me instructions that you was to stay here as a sort of thank you and I'll be here, too, and Phyllis, who's worked here for years."

I look down at my smart dress, feeling like the Cinderella of the fairy stories that my grandma would tell me about. This is the second time my hopes of a better standing in life have been cruelly snatched away, but a faint glimmer still exists that I might get an opportunity to see just a few more of the famous London sights I'd only ever seen in illustrations from old faded newspapers. I still need to know more, so ask about the current owner of this house.

"Now that'll be the Dowager Countess. She still hasn't got over the sudden death of her husband. Poor man's heart just gave out when they were staying here, and she doesn't want to come back to all those nasty memories. That's why she's glad to let her friends come and use the house in her absence. We've been told she's taking the sea air at some fancy French resort and she won't be back for five months. So your Lord fixed it with her to stop here whilst he finalised arrangements about his sister, seeing as he is currently having work done on his place."

I'm rather overcome with all this additional information that helps me to understand, but I press one further question from her.

"Can you tell me about Lady Gressingham as I can't recall ever having seen her?"

Mrs Blake laughs, then rises to bring over the large teapot. "Time for another cup and I'll maybe I'll fill you in with what I know!"

Chapter 26
London

This morning has all been a bit overwhelming with the shock of hearing how Lady Louisa has been whisked away so suddenly, and of the inevitable consequences that will now affect me. I'm still reeling at finding out that this is not Lord Gressingham's London home, and cannot understand why I've been granted a few days grace to use this grand house in his absence. Although it makes me feel very important, I am bracing myself for the day when I am ordered to return to Branswick Hall, and all this will feel like a dream that has just evaporated.

Today Mrs Blake has offered to show me some of the local sights. As the morning already feels warm with the fierce sun blazing down, I return to my little bedroom to change out of my heavy uniform clothes. I feel bold enough to wear the one special lemon muslin dress that I'd been given by Miss Ophelia. Before doing so I was eager to look into the rooms where I had last sat with the stricken lady, but I soon discover that the interconnecting door from my room is now firmly locked. I go into the corridor, but even there I realise that entry to her suite is barred, so I am none the wiser as to their state.

I busy myself getting ready, then with one more glimpse at the hand mirror, I adjust my straw hat and can't somehow believe what I am looking at. With my hair now much longer, it is hanging in ringlets at the back and I realise my face looks much fuller. I break into a smile and can't resist saying aloud,

"Why hello, Miss Florence! Aren't you the grand lady!"

It would be even more comforting to hear my sister Lizzie telling me that I look grown up, but it saddens me that when my birthday comes in two days' time and I reach the grand age of eighteen there will be no family messages or little gifts nor any way to mark the special day. It makes me yearn for home and the warmth of family life. Sighing, I replace the mirror and put those thoughts behind me as I set off to find Mrs Blake in readiness for my adventure.

I don't think I would ever have the nerve to walk along these London streets by myself and am truly grateful to have the companionship of one who knows them well. Mrs Blake is chatting continually and insists I call her Mary. She points out certain places, then baffles me with a string of the select names of their owners. I am simply awestruck by the towering houses we pass, with their grand steps and double doors, yet equally aghast as we look down some smaller alleys where the stench is rising from dirt piles. Seeing those run-down houses in such close proximity to the grand buildings is unbelievable. Even worse is the state of the ragged children I see sitting around on the ground.

I see true poverty and can't help but compare my own village life, where however poor we might have felt, we are rich by comparison to all of this.

"We're just coming up to the busy Oxford Street and now you will see the crowds! Used to be the old Roman road that led out from the city. You best hang on to my arm or you might get lost!"

Her offer is definitely welcome as I feel quite scared with the noises all around me. So many well-dressed folk are strutting proudly along the wide pavement, but even so, I notice they often bump into each other. Now I've only ever seen a top hat once before. It was worn when our town mayor arrived one year to open the summer fair in Felborough, but here they are worn by nearly every gentleman. I have to chuckle as they remind me of little chimney pots. But they are not so striking as the hats worn by the ladies as they walk along, creations of lace and fine fabrics that are swathed upon their heads, so wide they could easily be knocked askew in that busy crowd. There is so much activity all around I hardly know where to look. The actual road is heaving with an assortment of strange horse-drawn carts from which a towering vehicle sudden veers near the kerb, its wheels thundering as the panting horses pull it to a halt and I come face to face with my first London omnibus. It is crammed full of folk with a deck on the top from where smiling faces are peering down at the crowded pavement. Just like the picture in my little sister's scrapbook, I think, but so unusual and I'm fascinated by its circular staircase at the rear. I'm cheered to note that one of the young girls sitting up top is also wearing a straw boater and that pleases me for I smile and can't stop myself pausing and waving to her.

Mary Blake looks mystified at my behaviour and urges me along as she has an errand to run. What strikes me as odd are the number of unaccompanied ladies who stride purposefully along and make their way into the shops. I learn that this special area on the street caters solely for the needs of women and as such they feel secure to go in and shop alone. Hanging on to her arm, I certainly don't feel safe yet. I do not have the courage to let go while she makes her purchases and it is with some relief that I step outside again into the open air.

Now the mass of people seems even thicker and I feel myself starting to panic, so am quite reassured as Mary steers me back the way we had come. There are countless shop windows, each filled with a display of current London fashions, so ornate and colourful I can only gasp at their beauty as I pass by. At one junction of the road, Mary points out a large gap between the shops and I'm told that is to be the new train station that will soon be opening. When she explains that there are trains running beneath the ground, I do think at first she is teasing me, for surely that cannot be right, yet apparently it happens. I can't but wonder how many more startling revelations there will be on this outing.

As we cut away from the main thoroughfare it quietens down and I can now hear the sparrows chirruping up in the trees. We pass by a queue of young men who are waiting jovially outside a church hall. Some are smoking and others chatting or laughing out aloud as they joke together. One of them startles me by calling out:

""Ello, darling! You're a sight for sore eyes!"

I tilt my head down, not liking his tone of voice, but in doing so I trip as my foot catches the corner of a large placard upon which is written the heading, JOIN UP HERE. Had I not been hanging on to Mary's arm I think it would have ended in a bad fall, but luckily I managed to stay upright, if a little shaken by the experience. As we turn a final corner, the sight of the familiar frontages in Upper Brook Street finally allow me to breathe easier, but I do not completely relax until I hear the sturdy door close behind me.

This has been a whirlwind of a morning where at times I've felt out of my depth, totally bemused by all the strange sights, but also yearning for the quiet country life I know so well and that I realise I'm missing so badly. To express my thanks to Mrs Mary, as I prefer to address her, I insist on cooking a meal this evening. I watch as she throws back her head and gives a hearty laugh.

"Well it won't take much to put a cold ham salad together, so you'll be spared that, me dear!"

"Well, would it be possible for me to make an apple pie by way of thanks for taking me along with you today? If truth be told, I'd welcome a chance to be working again in a kitchen, somewhere I feel comfortable with what I know best."

In the future I would look back upon this day as one of those memorable times, with all the new experiences and wonders I had seen, plus the warm friendship of this kind-hearted woman who chats to me as if she'd known me all her life. She happily lets me delve into her cooking crocks and explains other intriguing facts as I go to work, flouring the wooden table top.

"Now, you was asking about them rowdy fellows we happened to pass. Well, they are answering a call for our young men to join the army, although if you ask me I reckon that's just signing up for a one-way ticket! I wouldn't want one of my sons to volunteer, that's if I had any sons."

The pause serves to indicate some sense of regret, but is swiftly put aside as she finishes her sentence.

"It beats me why we should be sending our fine lads out to Africa of all places! But they'll still queue up and join up, and it don't make no sense to me!"

It's only natural this makes me focus upon my own brothers. I'm now wondering if they would they ever be foolish enough to follow the crowd in search of adventure in a foreign land, without realising it could all end so badly. Maybe I should be thankful that at home we are often oblivious to world events, only learning of major events when word is spread amongst us throughout the villages.

Now sitting here, feeling full and content after our simple but filling meal, it feels wonderful to have this rare liberty and freedom from any authority. I'm blocking any thoughts of what might happen in the future, and find myself wishing these moments could be captured in a bottle, like the genie from those tales we are told as children.

Chapter 27
Motivation

I am awoken by a sudden rumble of thunder that sounds very close and continues for several seconds, to be followed by the sound of rain splattering upon my bedroom window. Now I've always has a strange fascination about storms and can't resist leaping out of bed to pull back the curtain. I can't explain why, but I feel compelled to watch and wait for the next lightning strike, even though it will send an uncontrollable shiver of fear from my head to my toes. I scan the brooding skies, holding my breath in readiness, knowing each time the flash will make me jump, and I shall think,

"Haha! You missed me! You can't scare me!"

As I watch, these notions suddenly seem slightly childish and I step back as the next flash splinters across the darkened morning sky. And then I remember with a sudden start that today is my birthday. What should be a day when I would be treated with love and kindness by my dear family will go unmarked and the sadness of that realisation brings me close to tears. I think about how Ma would probably fuss over me and would pronounce me a real young lady now I've turned eighteen, but all that is wishful thinking. It is with a heavy heart I wash and dress, knowing that this day will just pass without any acknowledgement and with that simple fact I am forced to put all such thoughts out of my mind.

A part of me is rather ashamed that I have not yet sent a message back home as to my current whereabouts. At least I can be thankful I was able to forewarn my family that I'd be working at His Lordship's London home. Now in light of recent events perhaps it is best I say nothing. After all it seems as if I'm soon to return to Branswick Hall and the thought of seeing them all again on my days off gives me a welcome inner buzz. Even so, I decide it would be only be courteous to send some kind of message to reassure Ma that all is well, so plan to ask Mrs Blake this morning how best to do this. I head for the stairs as yet another violent peal of thunder threatens to shake every brick in the building, and this time it does make me jump!

Walking into the large kitchen, I first spot Mrs Blake sat at the table with various envelopes lying there. She is intent on reading one of the letters. As she does so her head nods as she silently mouths the words as if to fix them firmly in her mind. Then she chortles and slumps back in her chair.

"Never a dull moment in this house! They come and they go, and it feels more like some upper-class lodging house and they all expect Mrs Sweet Fanny Adams Blake to be here! Still, I shouldn't complain "cos there's many a poor lass these days who doesn't have work and then they end up in the poor house."

It is only when she stops speaking I become aware of a man standing in the darkened recess where the pans are stored.

"All good for business Mrs B, and a boost to your little nest egg and retirement!"

It startles me as I immediately recognise the steady toneless voice of His Lordship's servant Withers. As he turns to face us, casually stirring a large cup of steaming tea, I fully expect to encounter one of his ritual glares, but I am pleasantly surprised to see him grinning.

"So how has our young Miss Gibbs been enjoying the high life then? You certainly made your mark girl! What was it he said to me? Something about letting you have a short time before he decides your future. If you ask me, he took a fancy to you, seen it all before. Well, I expect you've had a good old nose around, but don't get too smug! Things don't last for ever. So what's it to be next, heh?"

I start to feel threatened, but am spared from answering and grateful that Mrs Blake speaks out.

"Oh stop your teasing, Sidney! Poor lass was all of a dither after the dealings with Lady Louisa, and she did her very best to keep the insane woman calm. She's just having a well-earned break, that's all."

Waving her letter at me it's clear she wants to say more.

"Sid has just come over from Berkeley Square and he brought in today's post. This one is from the Countess advising me that her nephew and his family will be staying for the whole month of June, so I can see that'll be another hectic visit. It'll be endless picnic hampers to be packed for the races and I shall be run off my feet!"

The way she laughs tells me she'll rise to the occasion and be in her element.

"Maybe I could ask to stay on and help you, if that's possible."

I can see by the reaction on Wither's face this is a futile suggestion, as he strongly signals with a shaking head. He downs his tea and turns to face me.

"Afraid not. However, it seems you have a choice to make, so sit yourself down and listen."

The way he stresses the word *you* shoots alarm bells throughout my body, but I see the cook nod encouragingly at me, as if she has some former knowledge of what is to be revealed. So, taking a seat, I sit upright, trying to look confident with my head held high and my hands tightly interlinked to contain my apprehension.

"I'm here on specific orders of Lord Gressingham to ask you to work for his wife, Lady Caroline, but that it would mean moving her country home in Kent. However, he did say your previous place back at the Hall would still be available should you decline his offer."

Withers imparts this unexpected news, still gazing directly at me and I feel as a bolt of lightning has just struck me. There is an uneasy silence when I try to steady myself and think about the options presented to me.

"But what will I…"

There's such confusion crowding my mind that I fail to finish my sentence, and feel unable to take it all in. There's a certain sense of relief when I next hear him say, "He's giving you a day to make up your mind, although if that was me, I reckon I'd know which one I'd choose! Thanks for the tea, Mrs B. Best be getting back. Expect me the same time tomorrow."

I spend the next few hours deep in conversation with Mrs Blake, for, as I expected, she had been privy to the news before I came down. I felt sure with her wise advice I could decide which path to choose. But first I insist she keep her promise and tell me all she knows about Lady Caroline and her marriage to Lord Gressingham. Having been employed by both him and the Countess I felt she must be in the know. I learned that the first marriage was short lived and ended when his young wife died in childbirth and their infant daughter two days later. He had been grief stricken. Then ten years later he met this second wife at a country ball and had fallen head over heels in love with her. They were seen at all the grand houses and even royal palaces, and for a while they were known as the Golden Couple around town. Then over the passing years it become obvious that Lady Caroline was unable to bear him any children, and the relationship began to sour, so they chose to live separate lives, only reuniting when an occasion demanded their presence together. This news certainly explains why I had never seen a wife at Branswick Hall, yet it still gives me no indication as to her nature or personality. I feel numb and, in my frustration, call out: "This is not what I was expecting and I don't know what to do for the best. Oh, help me, please, Mary!"

Comforting arms are thrown around me as she suggests I take some time to fully consider my options, but she repeatedly throws in comments about what a wonderful opportunity this will be and that I should grab it with open arms.

"Why don't you go and sit up in the green room and take your time? Watch the skies clearing or the birds among the branches, and maybe that'll calm you and help you decide what's going to be for the best."

So I now find myself sitting at a desk overlooking the street, where the weak sunshine is slowly drying the rain puddles. I vow to push any decision-making to one side, for I am holding a postcard in my hand and it must be written today to send my news to my family. Mrs Blake had responded instantly to my request and I was handed a card and assured that I did not need to pay for it. Now the hardest decision is what I shall write. Just the very thought of seeing my brothers and sisters back in our cottage pulls me to take the safe option and return, but I am just as torn wondering if I have the nerve to face what could be an exciting future ahead. With a pencil I carefully write the address.

Family Gibbs, Higher Weldon. Beds.

I turn the card over and the empty side seems to reflect how I feel. I think hard but am a coward as I write the simplest of messages.

Hope you are all well, as I am, too.
Love, Flo.

Holding it to my lips I kiss one edge and know that tears are building once more. Through misty eyes I look around me, study the beautiful comfy chairs, listen to the slow steady beat of the ormolu clock above the fireplace, all the while savouring the grandeur of the room. Then a sudden shaft of sunlight gleams through the window and forces me to look outside, where I see a glorious rainbow above the rooftops. It's like a special sign and I feel energised by its vivid colours. My mind is made up! I offer a silent prayer of thanks for what might turn out to be the best birthday present I've ever received.

Chapter 28
Acceptance

I spent a restless night, tossing over what had been offered to me, one minute sure of myself, the next having multiple doubts as to the reality of another move that would take me even further away from my family roots. And yet the excitement of the unknown was urging me to go ahead. When I finally slept it was accompanied by a jumble of senseless dreams in which my sisters were crying at a funeral, yet my brothers were riding with me in an open-top landau. Dressed in strange uniforms, they were waving enthusiastically as we passed by the cortège and the sheer absurdity of the dream forced me to wake with a jolt. I steadied myself recalling the wise words of my great-grandpa who would cradle me as a small child when I had woken from a scary dream and would cry out.

He would calmly say, "Hush now, it's just the angels pulling your silly thoughts into the sky and turning them into rain clouds. Are you ready to blow them away?"

That homely image of us puffing the imaginary clouds still amuses and helps dispel my current anxiety.

True to his word, Withers arrives just as predicted. I barely have a chance to finish eating my bread when he breezes through the hallway looking none too pleased, brushing aside Mrs Blake's generous offer of breakfast.

"Right, cab's waiting. Are you ready to come or do I return without you?"

Hearing this snappy command, I begin to realise that he is showing a distinct level of disapproval and so I stand upright to face him, head held high whilst fixing my eyes directly at his ill-tempered face. This pause has its desired effect as he looks away.

"His Lordship didn't really expect you to agree to come, but you will be required to return to the Hall with us when we leave tomorrow."

Searching for words, I am urged on as Mrs Blake gestures with her hands, urging me to speak up.

"How very kind of you, Withers, to call for me. I just need a few moments and I shall be ready to travel with you. Now, will I be required to bring my belongings today?"

I'm rather proud of myself for showing such poise and highly amused to watch as Withers stares back in disbelief. Perhaps knowing I am now eighteen has emboldened me speak so forcefully and I feel no shame. He does not reply.

Mrs Blake takes charge and I realise I shall miss her kind mothering nature, but she can understand I want to better myself and this might be the way forward.

"Don't you go worrying about your effects; that'll all be sorted for you when the carter calls tomorrow. Go on, it's your big day and win them over with your lovely smile!"

The short ride in a hansom cab passes so swiftly that I fail to even look at the scene as it flashes by, simply staring down at the scuffed floor. Then it all seems a blur of activity as I was ushered into another imposing house and through into small parlour where I was ordered to wait. My attention is drawn towards some travelling trunks and two suitcases stacked along one of the walls, but I have no time to look further as the door opens and Lord Gressingham walks in, followed by Withers. He stands discreetly by the door as His Lordship approaches me. Strangely, I feel quite at ease, perhaps because I warm to seeing a familiar face – or is it his jovial look that inspires my confidence? I nod graciously, acknowledging his presence.

"M'Lord."

All he does is to throw back his head with a hearty laugh.

"So you came? Still the feisty Florence, I see! Well, it's not my decision as to your future. I shall leave that to my wife. Follow Withers and he will take you to her rooms."

I hesitate, expecting him to leave first, but he strolls over towards the bureau and I'm beckoned by his valet. What I find most heart-warming are the poignant comments I hear him quietly say as I pass.

"Don't blame yourself. She thought the world of you."

Reminders of the poor lady, now incarcerated, serve to unsettle me, but I realise in other ways it has opened a door into a far different world, even if it is now a leap into the unknown for me.

My first encounter with Lady Caroline was to take place in a darkened corridor as I was following Withers. This elegant vision appeared around a corner and took my breath away. She was a short lady, wearing a startling dress and bolero in a beautiful shade of olive green. Not only were there yards of lace adorning across the bodice, but she also she wore a very wide brimmed hat with swathes of cream chiffon that covered most of her face. She did not speak, but stood for a moment looking at me before moving on as I stepped aside.

Now I am patiently waiting in that same corridor to enter her private rooms. Mrs Blake has pre-warned me to expect a barrage of questions as to whether I would be suitable, but the mere fact is I still have no idea what my role is to be. A maid opens the door and I'm told to come in. I'm still admiring that stunning green dress as Lady Caroline stands with her back to me, and I note her shining brown hair, perfectly shaped, now it is revealed. Then I try not to gasp as she turns to face me, but smile and politely bob before daring to add:

"It's a pleasure to meet you, M'Lady."

I find myself looking at a whitened face that reminds me of a clown I'd once seen walking the streets as he advertised a forthcoming circus. I can see the makeup she has applied is far too pale and does her no favour, but it does not detract from her deep brown eyes that are looking earnestly at me. I certainly don't expect the flow of words that ensue or the kind way in which she rushes up to me and grasps my gloved hands.

"I've heard so much about you! Come and sit down with me and tell me all about yourself."

I'm pulled to sit alongside her upon a long, half-backed seat, not sure if this is the correct behaviour on her part or even mine.

"William has spoken well of you and your kindness to my unfortunate sister-in-law, and it was he who suggested you could be the perfect replacement now my dearest Beauvais has had to leave me. I thought she'd be with me forever, but she was too fond of her young man and when he inherited money she gave her notice and has gone off with him, leaving me all alone without a good and trusty maid!"

Her animated nature shines through the pale mask, causing me to think about what I have learnt of her previous misfortunes in life. In a similar way to the stricken Lady Louisa, I see a lonely soul who craves for friendship. Now I will just bide my time and wait for her to speak.

"Did you ever meet Beauvais? Oh, of course you wouldn't, how silly of me! She came to me from France over ten years ago, and advised me on choosing the latest Paris fashions that are just *so* superior to English designs. Have you ever been to France?"

She pulls away and there's an awkward silence as her hand moves to cover her mouth as if in shame.

"Forgive me for being so rude, but I've forgotten what they call you."

"My name is Gibbs, M'Lady, Florence Gibbs, and I have never been to France or to many parts of this country."

It's as if she is waiting for me to continue so I feel it pertinent to add, "Travelling to this great city has been my first big adventure and I shall always be grateful for that opportunity."

By omitting any further details regarding my humble beginnings I rather hope this gives a good impression, as something inside is telling me I may well be taking the place of Beauvais within Her Ladyship's household.

"Gibbs, you say? Oh good gracious, no! That won't do, it sounds too English. You shall be Florence!"

She pronounces it in a strange manner so that it rhymes with the word sconce. Now I can see there are four or five of these elaborately carved china fittings on the walls of that room, obviously of French design, so I begin to understand her obsession with that foreign country. I'm flattered as she leans towards me and practically begs me to travel with her.

"Do say you'll come with me, Florence. It's so much nicer being near the coast than here in London. I can't wait to feel the bracing sea air again."

She picks up a silver bell from the table and rings for a housemaid. I wonder if this is a signal for me to take my leave and move slightly forward on the seat.

"Oh no, please stay. We shall take tea and talk so that I can hear about your talents and get to know you!"

Nothing has prepared me for such an unusual meeting where I have yet to be officially offered the position of her personal maid. It's as if it were a done deal, prearranged by Lord Gressingham himself. I'm buoyed up as I think what my dear grandmother might have aptly said in this situation: "Fait accompli!"

Just for a fraction of a second it makes me think about everyone at home, knowing all too well it will be quite some time before I get to see them all again. But I want them to be proud of me and I promise myself that I will write to them more regularly. Now is my chance to impress this lady, for in my heart I already feel a rapport with her and am sure I can serve to the best of my abilities.

Chapter 29
Coast

The view from my large attic bedroom is beyond my wildest dreams, for each day I look out on the wide expanse of sea as it shifts and changes colour. It is totally awe-inspiring watching how the wind constantly tosses up the white flecks of spray or drives into the sails of the boats causing them to tilt alarmingly so that I sometimes fear for the safety of their crew. I'm sitting here now, by an open window, with every intention of writing a letter to Ma and Pa, hoping I can convey an image of this invigorating scene. It is so different from the stillness of the countryside where I was raised, where the silence is only broken by the sounds of birds or farm cattle, or periods of wild weather. I have so much to tell them and hardly know where to begin.

True to His Lordship's word, I have been taken on as a replacement for Beauvais and now serve Lady Caroline as her personal maid. This had been a big step into the unknown, but I convinced myself that I would be perfectly capable of so many of the tasks required of me, and would be a willing learner. I find her to be a very pleasant lady, who wants to happily engage in conversation. Once it had been agreed that I would accompany her on her return, it was only on our train journey down to Kent that she seemed to formally question me as if to get to know me better. She listened as I gave brief details of my life in the country, carefully omitting the fact I was previously employed purely as a cook's help, but that I had served both Miss Ophelia and Lady Louisa without any complaints. I wisely added that I was grateful for this wonderful opportunity to serve Her Ladyship and would be willing to learn any new skills as she so desired. I hoped that I had conveyed a confident portrayal of myself.

Likewise, I warmed to her as she spoke of her likes and dislikes and I got a sense that I was being eagerly welcomed into her household. I do recall how she laughed when I mentioned I was looking forward to seeing her country home and did wonder why. It struck me as odd that the green fields had given way to a built-up area as our train appeared to be heading into a town. We had transferred to an awaiting horse-drawn carriage and only then was I to discover on arrival that her country home was in fact an elegant town house, one of many in a crescent that stood high on a cliff face, overlooking the sea. It was quite a shock seeing such a wide expanse of water for my very first time that I almost forgot my manners as I stood there and gazed open mouthed at its vastness.

I'll never forget her first words as she was assisted down from the carriage and stood there too, a broad smile breaking over her pallid face.

"Isn't it simply heavenly? I feel alive when I come back here and I can see its sheer beauty has captured your heart already!"

Now with these thoughts uppermost in my head I concentrate on the sheet of paper and carefully write the following words.

Dear family,

I am now living in the pretty seaside town of Folkestone in Kent. I am personal maid to Lady Gressingham and she treats me very well. She insists I walk with her each day and we stroll along the paths that are high above the cliffs and watch the boats as they leave or enter the fishing harbour. The sea changes every day and is so breath-taking to look at. Oh, I wish you could be here to see it all. Have you received my wages this month as was arranged? I miss you so much. I send love to Ma and Pa and everybody, until we can meet again.

From Florence

With the letter now secure in an envelope, I hope my news will enlighten them as to my whereabouts and put their minds at rest. I have this treasured hour to myself as Lady Caroline has visitors today. In my room there is a large framed mirror attached to one wall where I pause to look at myself. I still can't quite believe that I'm wearing such a rich brown dress that perfectly matches my hair and I find that most satisfying. Unlike the previous outfits I had worn at Branswick Hall, these have been especially ordered for me. The dress fits perfectly, made of a light material for the summer months. Even the white aprons I wear are embellished with lace panels that run from the neck to the bottom. I stand there feeling rather grand, checking that my hair is secure in its tight bun at the back before fixing on my small cap. It has no basic function of covering my hair, but simply looks very impressive. I could almost imagine I was wearing a grand bejewelled tiara. I turn away feeling slightly ashamed of these thoughts. I know I would never dare mention any of this in my letter for fear it would make my sisters jealous of my status. I head for the door and begin to descend the stairs, half skipping with happiness and still clutching my letter.

Mrs Heath is the trusted housekeeper here and always makes me smile with her outright comments, but even more so her mannerisms when she is in the safety of her own private room. Although I knock first, and hear her clipped tone as she calls aloud, "Enter!", she then lets down her guard when I pop my head around the door. So I now find her looking hot and bothered with her legs splayed wide open whilst she fans herself with a rolled-up newspaper.

"Phew! I can see we're heading for a scorcher of a month. Flaming June's arrived all right - what I'd give for a sea breeze right now!"

I'm so grateful for the caring way she treated me on my arrival. It took me completely by surprise to find her to be the complete opposite of Mrs Baynton, who kept very strict rules at the Hall, ever keeping a watchful eye on all the private lives of the staff. I do suspect this household is run very differently with Lady Caroline in charge. I think she could see I was inexperienced and unsure of my role, so I am indebted to her for the guidance and advice she has since given me.

"Just take things at your pace, my dear; no point in rushing around for anything. It makes a change from the way that little French madam used to dart around, trying to do things so fast and then getting in a fair old muddle. It was hardly worth her bother! Still, she worked hard and we were all sorry she decided to go."

Hearing that makes me feel as if I'm a poor replacement. Perhaps the way I hang my head or fact that I am biting my lip causes Mrs Heath to sit upright and firmly state,

"But Her Ladyship is thrilled that you wanted to come and I've not seen her so happy for months! Now, are you wanting that letter posted? Just leave it in the wooden box in the hallway. Levison will take the post down later this afternoon."

"How about if we just go outside for a few minutes to feel the breeze, Mrs Heath? That should cool you down."

"Love to, my dear, but I'm waiting on Lady Maud to return so I'd better not. Of course you've yet to meet Her Ladyship's sister, haven't you? She has the suite on the second floor, but spends most of her time staying with her friends all around the country. Particularly fond of some stately home up in Berkshire I've heard. They do that you know, just move into each other's homes for what they call the season. I don't expect she'll be here for very long. Too fond of her parties and the horses. She used to ride herself; well, they both did until Lady Caroline had her bad fall. It upset them both and I don't think they ever got back on a horse after that incident."

I learn more from these informal chats that helps build a fuller picture of my employer and am now highly curious about the prospect of meeting her sister, so continue my questioning.

"I didn't understand why I was staying in a house that didn't belong to Lord Gressingham, but now I realise that's how they live their lives, so very different from us. So will I be called upon to assist with this lady?"

I watch as the housekeeper vehemently shakes her sweaty head.

"Good Lord no! She's one of a kind. You'll see!"

I take my leave, desperate to look once more at the changing sea and relish my free time. There are always little groups promenading along the paths, and today I notice some young ladies in their fancy floral dresses who choose to walk alone and that makes me feel safe as I watch them pass by. They look very grand, twirling their lace parasols to shade themselves and several of them smile as they pass by. I start to believe that there is a certain kind of magic when you are by the sea, for I find myself with a permanent smile on my face. I've yet to venture further down nearer to the bustling harbour, having only seen it from the carriage when I first arrived. As I look out to sea, I spot a large steamboat heading towards the harbour mouth, its trail of smoke drifting gently up like a waving banner. It is such an outstanding sight to behold and I try to imagine what it must feel like being on board. My only experience of being on the water was that other magical time when I was in a rowing boat on the lake, quite fearful of falling in the water yet charmed by the beauty of the occasion. I sigh, but still think fondly of Miss Ophelia, although I doubt we shall ever meet again.

Chapter 30
Trust

Caroline watches from her bed, carefully shielding her face with the covers and waiting for the housemaid to leave the room with her breakfast tray. I have my bathing duties to organise with several jugs of hot water that have been brought to the room. It is so satisfying to add the perfumed rose water and swish it gently in readiness for Her Ladyship's bath. I realise from her rare comments that she still misses the pert antics of her former maid, who I gather was forever chattering or sighing over the silliest thing. However, it gratifies me to hear how pleased she is with the calm gentle way that I go about my duties and I sense she is more than happy with my work. I do find it rather odd that she waits patiently each morning until I leave the room before she starts to bathe, then dress and prepare herself for the coming day. I often wonder what secret she is hiding.

As I emerge from the adjacent bathroom I stand discreetly by the door, slightly embarrassed at seeing my mistress half hidden in her bed, with just her eyes peeping over the top of the covers.

"Your bath is ready M'Lady, and there is a jug of cold water should it prove too hot for you. The skies are very blue today and it is warming up already. I've laid out the dress as you requested. Is there anything else I can get for you?" I wait patiently for her response whilst mentally checking everything is to order.

"That will be all, thank you. Oh, just a thought, can you find those sweet little pink shoes that match so perfectly? They are so comfortable to wear and if it is as pleasant out as you have indicated, I'd very much like to take a stroll before the real heat of the day. We shall take the air together!"

I do as she bids, placing the shoes alongside the chair, then nod as I close the door with its customary click. The rustle of bedclothes can be heard as her Ladyship now rises to take her morning bath and I head for the stairs for a few precious moments. Caroline sinks low in the water and does not care that her wet hair is floating like the seaweed on the tide. She talks to herself in these private moments for she feels that it helps to clear her troubled thoughts.

"Oh Caro, Caro! Why can't I say anything? She'll understand, I know she will. She won't judge me. Such a sweet girl, and we have similar thoughts. She is almost like a sister to me."

The image of her true sister Maud, rears in her mind, and serves to dampen any pleasant feelings she has just experienced. The household were on alert to expect her arrival yesterday afternoon, and were none too happy being kept waiting the whole day. Lady Maud finally put in an appearance as the clocks were striking ten. She had been travelling alone and looked decidedly flustered. She had dismissed any offers of food or help and simply bolted straight to her rooms demanding her usual bedtime drink and that she was not to be disturbed. Caroline has yet to greet her sister and realises she must be on her guard to maintain a civility when they meet this morning.

The soft towels are comforting to her as she pats herself dry and briskly rubs her damp hair before shaking it from side to side until she feels totally invigorated. From her bay window she watches some early risers as they walk by, one lady holding fast to her summer hat in the morning breeze. She dresses eagerly in the desire to be doing likewise at the earliest opportunity. Normally she does not ring for me until she has sat and applied her face powder, and only then does she feel ready for her hair to be brushed and styled for the day.

I had been enjoying a hot drink downstairs with Mrs Heath when Levison suddenly appeared and silently handed over a sealed letter addressed to Caroline but with large words printed across the top: FOR IMMEDIATE ATTENTION!

"You better take that up straight away, Florence. I reckon that's come from her sister Maud! Looks like her writing. I wonder what's so important?"

I'm not sure if I should interrupt the bathing session, but do as I am bid and return to the upper floor. It takes some nerve to make myself knock on the door and call out, "I've an urgent message M'Lady, from the Lady Maud."

There is no response so I take it upon myself to open the door and accept the consequences of my actions.

"Beg pardon for interrupting M'Lady, but I was ordered to deliver this note immediately."

Lady Caroline is dressed and standing by her dressing table with her back to me. I watch her hesitate before she turns to face me and reluctantly takes the letter from my hand.

"Thank you, Florence. As you can now see, this is the burden I've had to bear since childhood and one I will always need to disguise. I wouldn't wish this on anyone."

I finally begin to understand as I see the vivid red strawberry birthmark that stretches down one side of Lady Caroline's face. It clearly explains her need for the creams and powders she uses so heavily, but it also points the way for me to help her make better use of the colouring. It does not shock or embarrass me, but I hasten to add, "My cousin Alice has a similar mark on one of her cheeks and we all say she has been blessed by the Lord and that it marks her out for special things in her life."

I hope these words will allay any deep-seated issues my mistress might hold. I watch as she exhales and it is clear to see the relief on her face now that her secret is revealed. In fact, I sense she feels somewhat foolish for having kept it from me. She waves the letter in the air, still unopened.

"I suppose this is one of her ridiculous demands, and so like Maud to warrant our attention."

I have heard one or two odd details from the staff about Lady Maud and am curious to meet her. I watch as Caroline reads from the single sheet, then throws the paper to the floor in disgust.

"Always asking for my money for some of her latest schemes, but why she feels this is urgent is beyond my thinking! Says she needs a bicycle as she left hers at her friend's house. The very thought of any lady mounted on those unwieldy contraptions sends my heart all of a quiver, don't you agree Florence?"

I haven't the heart to disagree but this has evoked a few memories and I find myself smiling. Caroline is not to know that the mere mention of a bicycle has awakened wonderful thoughts of Albert and the way he would he ride along, daring to do so without touching the handlebars in order to impress me.

"Several of the lads back at home have saved their money and bought bicycles M'Lady. They save so much time in travelling."

I think it best not to say that all the girls in the village had taken a turn trying to ride. Some had succeeded but I had wobbled and quickly dismounted, fearing my skirt would become entangled.

"I think they will become very popular but our clothes are not very suitable to wear. I have heard that sometimes the ladies hitch up their long skirts to make it more comfortable as they ride."

Lady Caroline is now laughing, quite forgetful of her looks. She sits down and picks up the hairbrush as if to signal me to resume my duties.

"I suppose I'd better warn you that my sister is rather an unconventional lady. Do not be alarmed by her appearance when you meet her; she has this compulsion to be different and to shock people. She was always like that, even as a small

144

child, forever climbing trees in our orchard. Our poor dear Mother tried her best to see she was clothed in pretty dresses but they were continually torn or Maud would pull them off and run half naked around the garden. Do you have sisters, Florence?"

She pauses as she enjoys the feel of the brush gliding through her hair, then indicates how she'd like it swept up high to keep her cool. I have done this before but need to concentrate on making sure the grips are firmly secure, so do not immediately answer.

"Maybe you have brothers instead? There's just Maud and myself, and she's all I've got left of family, so I feel bound to tolerate her strange ways."

As I stand back and hold the hand mirror for her to view the results of my work, she seems pleased with my efforts. Replacing the silver brush, I am glad of the opportunity to talk about my siblings for I do so miss them.

"I have four sisters and four brothers M'Lady. All so very different but we have been taught to be kind to each other and respect our differences."

Uppermost in my thoughts are Harriet and of her disappearance. I am still hoping to hear news by return of post now the family have been informed of my new address.

"Mary is my youngest sister, and she too can be a bit wild, forever roaming the countryside and getting into scrapes. That's how some people are M'Lady and we can't change them."

"You have a very wise head on young shoulders. What age are you, Florence? I feel I must get to know you better." Lady Caroline turns on her chair and looks directly at me. "Thank you for not averting your face when you saw mine. When I was younger, the mark was far paler and did not bother me but as the years have passed it has darkened significantly. Perhaps you now understand my obsession with the powders I use. Beauvais knew just how to blend the creams but since she left, I seem unable to achieve the same effect."

145

It is humbling to hear such confessions and I'm quick to ask if I can now help with the applications. I feel sure a warmer colouring would be far more suitable but applied more sparingly.

"I'd be happy to help you, M'Lady. I shall see you look perfect for our little stroll, that's if you are still wanting to go out?"

That small enticement has the desired effect as Caroline grins.

"Work your magic, young Florence and we shall indeed strut out in our finery!"

Now is not the time to consider how my brown dress can be classified as finery, for I set to work in anticipation of walking alongside Lady Caroline, and being proud to do so.

Chapter 31
Encounter

I have to admit that when I first set eyes on Lady Maud, I took an instant dislike to her. Reverend Henderson once admonished me for saying I could judge what a person was like at first sight. He said we should be patient and talk with them before coming to those conclusions. But I know from past experience my initial reactions are always right. It wasn't the way she had her hair harshly swept to the back of her head, making her look extremely masculine, or the way her steely eyes focused on us, but simply the manner in which she addressed her sister. Lady Caroline was so pleased after I had finished her makeup she became eager to be walking out in the hope she would meet up with her acquaintances. Then as we were leaving the house, briefly dazzled by the brilliant sunshine as it reflected from the flight of stone steps, Maud was there, standing on the path and barring our way. I now understand why she has been labelled as odd, for she is wrapped in a deep purple velvet cape, completely unsuited for the heat of the day. She does not smile, but glares at her sister in her pretty outfit.

"You never change, do you? Still the little madam flaunting your wealth with never a care for my needs! I assume you received my note?"

I am quite taken aback at the tirade of words, and find it hard to see any sibling affection or resemblance on that hard-set face. Lady Caroline does not flinch but looks around, checking no one is in the vicinity before speaking in a low voice.

"This is not a suitable place for a conversation, Maud. I will speak with you in my rooms at three o'clock. Now kindly let us pass."

With that she grabs my arm and we walk away. I am all too aware of the cursory look I am given as I hurry past this wild lady and I find it quite unnerving. The encounter has obviously upset M'Lady too as she insists on linking her arm through mine as we cross the grassy area, and I sense this is for moral support while she comes to terms with the unsavoury incident. We walk for a short time in silence and it gives me time to reflect on how fortunate I am to know the love of my family and be so thankful they are sane human beings. To encounter yet another unsteady character after my recent dealings with Lady Louisa now alarms me. I begin to wonder if madness is more likely to occur amongst those high born and then I remember poor Thomas. Well, he may be simple minded, but thank goodness he'll never be labelled as mad.

The sun beams down on us and somehow puts the world to rights. There are plenty more folk out and about this morning. It gladdens me when Lady Caroline is greeted by a family that she knows well, for I feel her regaining confidence as they laugh and chatter. I will step back at a respectful distance so do not hear their private conversations. Today I am introduced to their personal maid, a reserved little soul who seems reluctant to talk to me, other than to say her name.

"Bertha, but called Parsons."

I try to engage her in conversation, thinking how pleasant it would be to meet at a future date.

"Hello, I'm Florence Gibbs and I've only be here for a few weeks, but I just love it here, with the view overlooking the sea. Have you lived here long?"

"Three years."

She clearly does not want to share any further information and when I ask her if she can recommend things I could visit in the town, all she does is to shake her head. "Don't know."

Clearly there is no feeling of rapport between us and I'm thankful to see gestures of farewell as the family prepare to continue their walk signifying out departure.

"Charming people, the Langhams! They rent a property for two months each summer and have been so kind to me, inviting me to join them on trips around the neighbouring countryside." Lady Caroline has paused as the path diverges and heads down a wooded slope on its way to the lowered levels of the cliff.

"I have come to the conclusion that friends are far more important in life than those we count as family. Don't you agree, Florence? Now, shall we brave the slopes or stay along the top?"

It amuses me that I am being asked to choose our route, so make the quick decision to remain walking on the level where we can benefit from the cooling draughts of air that come from below. That last statement has got me puzzling about her marriage to Lord Gressingham and I toss over in my mind how best to raise the subject without giving offence.

"If you look ahead, M'Lady, there is an empty seat just a little further along should you feel the need for a short rest and it will afford a great view out to sea."

She stops and looks around and then her response takes me by surprise.

"I shall race you there!"

And true to her words she releases my arm and scurries towards the bench like a child racing to retrieve a ball. Her actions strike me as quite funny and I can't help but stand and laugh. I'm rather glad there are no other walkers near us to witness what has just occurred. It is a very special moment for me as I feel that I've been fully accepted as the replacement for Beauvais. Now she is patting the metal bench inviting me to sit alongside her. I hope this will pave the way for me to talk freely with her.

"I hope you don't mind me saying, but I am very grateful that Lord Gressingham arranged this post for me."

149

There is an uncomfortable silence as Caroline sits deep in thought. It is broken by the solitary scream of an overhead tern, hovering on the thermals of air and we both look upwards to observe its antics. Perhaps I have touched a raw nerve and decide to say no more. As I look beyond the cliff edge at the vastness of the sea I can almost imagine there is land in the distance, but convince myself it is probably a cloud formation on the horizon. But I am not alone in those thoughts for in a similar vein she sparks into life, her hand pointing ahead.

"Look! That's the coastline of France, so near yet so far. One day Florence, one day. And now I shall head back, not that I'm looking forward to this afternoon!"

It is only a five-minute stroll back to the crescent and I follow in her footsteps. Lady Caroline is humming softly to herself, sometimes leaning over to randomly pluck the odd leaf or two for no apparent reason and deep in thought. We are about to head for her home when she moves closer to me.

"I loved him very much you know, but sometimes relationships crumble, for one reason or another."

She has taken hold of my hand and is now holding it alongside her cheek by way of explanation.

"Have you ever loved someone deeply, Florence? It still pains me to think what happened, but William has been very generous in providing for me and for that I'm grateful. I have a beautiful home by the sea, kind friends, and he chose to send you like an angel of mercy! Now, to brace myself in readiness of facing the wrath of my sister."

Lady Caroline holds up one corner of her dress and walks up the steps. I am imagining how my sister Sue would laugh so much if I told her I had been called an angel of mercy! It's a flattering thought, but I am more than satisfied that Her Ladyship has felt able to confide in me. My elderly grandmother used to say we all have a purpose in life and it was just the art of finding the right one that would make us happy. At this very moment as I follow her up the steps, I am more than content with this arrangement.

Chapter 32
Secrets

The domestic arrangements in this household are so different from the rigid hierarchy I had experienced back at the Hall. I still do not know who some of the staff are, for I am expected to take my meals in a private room, often on my own or in the company of the housekeeper. As there are no gentlemen residents, it appears we do not have a butler, but there is one footman who deals with certain orders, whilst Mrs Heath consults Her Ladyship about all other matters. I've yet to discover who Levison is, having only observed a couple of daily maids who work diligently but efficiently around the house. I have tried to engage them in conversation but they shy from any involvement in deference to my status. Those are the moments when I feel isolated and in crave a friendly face in which to confide or simply talk. In spite of that, I have become very fond of Lady Caroline and rather proud of the way I have adapted to her style of living. I am now of the opinion that her life is led in a very casual way and am convinced it is the sea effect that encourages a freedom that does not exist elsewhere.

She often chooses to go without a midday meal, asking only for fresh fruit to be brought to her rooms, but will always change for the evening meal. I can't imagine anyone relishing being alone at a long dining table, but I gather that is the done thing and there are many times when I know she has invited guests to dine with her, then I hear laughter and know she is enjoying herself. The arrival of Lady Maud last week cast a shadow over the household, all wary of her outbursts and reprimands. I know I overheard raised voices on two occasions, even that of the normally placid Lady Caroline who was heard to shout out, "I will NOT pay your debts! Try asking your beloved Isobel; I'm sure she'd oblige!"

I think they might have been the last words said between the two sisters, for we were told that Lady Maud had left early the next morning, as swiftly as she had arrived. You could almost feel the sense of relief from everyone, including M'Lady, although I observed she kept very silent for most of the day.

The weather has taken a turn for the worse, as short sharp showers buffet the window panes then evaporate as the sun streams through once more. We are not taking the air this afternoon. Instead, I am sitting sewing in an anteroom that was most probably a dressing room attached to a bedroom. I did once try the door, but found it locked. I like to come here as there is plenty of light for me to work by. One of the lace cuffs on her green dress has come loose and it pleases me to know I can repair it. I always find this activity quite soothing and pride myself on my workmanship. Deep in thought, I am startled by a small rap at the door and the following words: "A letter for you, Miss."

The young girl standing there, tray in hand, is unknown to me. She looks slightly awe struck. Then as I take the letter from the tray, she immediately turns and I watch as she speeds downstairs. I know from the spidery writing that it is a letter from my sister Lizzie and I am most eager to read it. Just holding the flimsy paper in my hand warms my heart as I scan the words, desperate for any news.

Dear Lizzie has kept her sentences as brief as she can so as to include news of everyone, thus I learn Henry still sees Ivy, Pa has a bad chest and Joe has sold more carvings. I read these little snippets of good news about the other members of my family who are thriving, but I feel slightly concerned to know my dear ma is having bad spells, which she calls The Change. Lizzie has written so much that the sheet of paper is already covered, so she has written the last few sentences at right angles. I have some trouble trying to make out her words, then what I decipher fills me with sadness. I read them in disbelief and with a great longing to be back with my family.

Harriet came home. She was very ill for a while. Ma does not know the whole story, but she was badly treated by Reggie Mason, covered in bruises.

I struggle to read the final words she has written across the lines, for they are even smaller but it explains all too vividly how she had lost her unborn child when thrown violently across the room. Lizzie had signed off with much love and three poignant words.

Ma mustn't know.

My sewing sits discarded as the tears begin to fall and I feel so helpless as I sit and grieve for her. Oh, my poor Harriet, you didn't deserve that. So, my suspicions had been correct all along, but even so it would have been a first grandchild for my parents and would no doubt have been loved, whatever the circumstances preceding its birth. Those final words she wrote now haunt me, though it means I finally know the truth. It is a relief to know Harriet is now safely home.

I find no joy in my sewing, but finish the job as quickly as I can, which is hard as my eyes keep filling with tears. I need to retreat to my attic room, where I wash and tidy myself in readiness before returning the mended dress to its closet. We have a prearranged pattern of raps when I knock on Her Ladyship's door, one she recognises and answers with a gentle call.

"Come."

Today she is sitting in a comfy padded chair. She holds a book in her hand but doesn't seem interested in it. Instead, she gazes out at the cliff tops and scans the ominous clouds that darken the sky, simultaneously running her fingers through the green fronds of an enormous potted palm tree that stands adjacent to her chair.

"I've repaired the cuff, M'Lady, so the dress is ready to be worn again."

I like to show my handiwork for her approval, but in doing so she detects the sadness from my reddened eyes.

"Oh, Florence, what is troubling you? Where are your lovely smiles today? Can I be of any help, my dear?"

Such well-meant kindness is too much for me to bear and I cannot stop myself from bursting into tears. I know this is deplorable behaviour, but it seems beyond my control. I am ordered to sit while Lady Caroline waits patiently for my tears to subside. In her presence I calm down, muttering profuse apologies for my behaviour that are instantly dismissed. She then encourages me to unburden my problems. I am more than grateful for the sympathetic way in which she listens to me, and soon regain my self-composure as I share my anxieties. I thank her and force a weak smile, but she is now lost in thought as if searching for the right thing to say. With a swift movement Lady Caroline suddenly rises, and stretches out her hand towards mine.

"Come with me. I'd like to share something with you."

She gently holds my hand and we move through into another smaller bedroom that shines with golden fabrics and has an inviting single bed piled high with a luxurious gold and lemon coverlet. I find it all intriguing until she points to a low chair in the corner. It is filled with white lace cushions and then I see the two lifelike baby china dolls that are nestled there. I've never seen anything so beautiful before and gasp.

"Oh, how simply wonderful! You must have had so much pleasure as a child playing with them, M'Lady."

I can't help but compare them to our simple but equally lovable ragdolls that my sisters and I shared. They have the most realistic moulded faces that look so lifelike and appealing, yet I sense they could be very fragile to handle. Lady Caroline shakes her head in denial, but it's her following words that leave me riveted to the floor.

"Florence, what has happened to your poor sister saddens me too, for I also know the heartbreak of losing children. Now, I want to you meet Pierre and Annabelle. I keep them as a

154

reminder of what might have been. Do not think unkindly of me when I tell you that there have been times when I would cradle them in my arms. I used to have this strange notion that I could breathe life into them; that's the effect such a loss can have upon a woman. Your sister will take a while before she begins to come to terms with losing her unborn child, but believe me, Florence, like so many others she will adjust to life as it moves forward."

It is humbling that she has revealed all this to me and I have to suppress the strong urge to hold her tight by way of thanks. She gently picks up the boy doll and adjusts his perky little cap before showing me the realistic china hands that peep from under the pale blue jacket.

"Aren't they simply divine? French dolls are the finest you can buy, and I have made this *ma passe-temps favori* since living here. I confess I do have others kept well wrapped in their boxes and will happily show you at some future time."

She giggles as if it is a naughty secret, but it is clear to me that she loves these objects. I notice the care she takes as she carefully lays the doll back on the chair. I follow her through the door, musing on her French words, which I make out to be our equivalent of "pastime" and am full of admiration for her honest remarks.

"Thank you for understanding, M'Lady. Will there be anything else?"

"No thank you, Florence. As there is no sign of the weather improving I shall just read today, but I intend to take you to the charming establishment in the town where these dolls are displayed. Now I suggest that next Tuesday, all being well, you accompany me and I will show you around. Who knows, I might be tempted to purchase yet another one!"

Chapter 33
Shop Window

True to her words, I am informed on the Tuesday morning that a carriage will be arriving to take us into the town just after eleven o'clock. A maid knocks and hands over the breakfast tray and I take it to her bedside. I do admire the way that Mrs Heath orders the inclusion of a single flower in a cut-glass vase. Today there is a delicate lemon rosebud along with a folded newspaper beside her dish of eggs and the silver jug.

"Shall I pour your coffee now, M'Lady, or will you wait?"

A headline on the paper has caught her attention so she does not answer my query.

"How strange! They are reporting that a giant balloon has been used in Germany to fly people in the sky! Apparently, it is so long it resembles a giant wurst. Whatever will they think of next!"

She laughs aloud and I find it amusing, too, although I have no idea what she is describing. Instead I am left with a strange image in mind of people hanging on to ropes and dangling beneath and it all sounds quite ridiculous. I seem to recall something my brother Joe had said last year as we were approaching the new century. He had predicted the world would change with new inventions, and machines would end up doing all the jobs and everything would move faster and faster and the world would go crazy! Pa had cuffed him and told him he was living in "cuckoo land" and we had all laughed. Now it appears that maybe the world is changing, as the papers confirm these predictions.

"Yes do pour, Florence – oh, and I think it would be appropriate if you wore one of your own dresses today. I want to introduce you to Monsieur Leroc who is the proprietor of the charming little shop we are to visit."

She smells the rosebud then picks up a fork. "My lemon dress today, please, with the white bolero and my white parasol. I think it will be another hot July day!"

I feel quite excited at the prospect of this visit and puzzle over what to wear amongst my limited selection, not wanting to appear foolish or out of place. I finally decide to go with a pale grey skirt topped with a cream blouse. It makes me look well presented as I twist and turn in front of my mirror and feel every bit a young lady. I have added a new yellow ribbon around my worn straw hat to brighten the look and hope this will not detract from Her Ladyship's fine clothes. A horse-drawn cab awaits us at the appointed time and that is a new experience, as I have to sit alongside Lady Caroline. I note that this cab balances on just two wheels and the rocking movement alarms me as we mount the steps. However, when in motion it steadies as we jog along to approach the shops in the town and it is a most pleasant ride. It pleases me to see Her Ladyship looking beautiful and I'm thankful the gentler shades of cream have worked their magic. I know I should feel lucky that my complexion is good. I have yet to need anything applied to my face, save a slight touch of reddening if my cheeks look wan. To have this daily routine is a chore she bravely accepts. She's even taught me a French saying that explains it perfectly. I have vague recollections of hearing it said by my grandmother when I was a child: *Il faut souffrir pour être belle.*

Back then I had no idea what it meant. Now I like the sound it makes. It has a rhythm you could sing to and seems to match the clopping of the hooves as we travel. But there is no time to continue with these thoughts as we draw up outside a row of shops and come to a halt. The sign above reads LA PETITE CRÈCHE in artistic swirls of cream against deep chocolate paintwork. To my eyes it looks extremely elegant and expensive.

157

The shop front has one small bow window, neatly draped with fine muslin curtains that just reveal a glimpse of three elegantly dressed dolls who are seated around a tiny table as if they are all taking afternoon tea. It tempts one to see more, for there is only one sweet face looking out whilst the other two have their backs to the window. Lady Caroline is intrigued, too, for she bends low to peer at the display.

"So clever how he positions them to entice you in for a better view! Ah, Monsieur Leroc! Bonjour! I have brought along Florence to see the wonderful creations you have on sale."

An elderly gentleman with a neat pointed beard has opened the door to allow our entry. He looks very dapper in a well-buttoned suit that sports a high wing collar and he clicks his heels together as he greets both of us, eager to bustle around a prospective customer. Their conversation is in French and highly animated so that I am unable to follow. Instead I look around at the boxes that line a shelf, each holding a perfect childlike doll as if they are sleeping in their cradles. I would dearly love to pick one up and examine their exquisitely made clothes and can't stop gazing at them. A movement to my right startles me as a masculine figure emerges from a rear door carrying another box, which he presents to Lady Caroline before revealing its contents.

"Oh, simply adorable! Come, Florence, I want you to see this delightful doll."

She addresses the man standing by her. "Does he have a name?"

"The one in this range is called Edouard. Such realistic modelling, don't you agree? We have been importing these from Germany."

There is something about that voice that sounds vaguely familiar, but I am too keen to take a look and hasten over. This one is so like a newborn child, with its eyes closed tight and soft looking cheeks that I can only marvel at the workmanship and whisper, "It's really beautiful, M'Lady."

It is only now as I step back that I realise who I am facing and my heart skips a beat with the shock of the confrontation. Our eyes lock in disbelief.

Monsieur Leroc turns to me and speaks hesitantly in a quaint accent.

"Allow me to introduce *mon fils*, Jean-Claude, who is our chief purchaser of these porcelain-headed dolls."

He smiles and points towards the rear part of the shop. "Perhaps you show Mam'selle…?"

Lady Caroline is deep in conversation and I can see she will be easily won over to make a purchase. I cannot refuse the invitation as Jean-Claude gestures for me to follow him to the rear of the shop and beyond. It is in the privacy of this small store room that he finally speaks in a barrage of excitable sentences.

"Florence? It is Florence, yes? Now let me see. A dear friend of young Ophelia, if I recall? This is a most pleasant surprise to meet again as our paths cross! And I believe you are living with our esteemed client, Lady Gressingham?"

For once I am lost for words, but being in his presence serves as a reminder of former times, even though it had been the briefest of meetings at the vicarage. His eyes sparkle behind the spectacles that he wears and he is smartly dressed and clean shaven, but what marks him out is the flamboyant cravat he wears today. Made of floral silk, it is tied like the bows that are occasionally seen adorning the rear of ladies' fashion. I am also aware of a pleasant aroma from a lotion he wears and it fascinates me to want to know him better. As my confidence returns, I am able to tell him that I am now appointed as a personal maid to Lady Caroline and how much I like being by the coast and living in Folkestone. Jean-Claude is keen to tell me about the business and I learn how he trades on the Continent importing these dolls for an admiring English clientele. He moves around showing me more of their treasures and I listen avidly as he goes into detail about their manufacture. The way he fixes his direct looks at me awakens

159

a feeling I can't quite explain and I am flattered by his attentions. I start to feel flustered so decide to make enquiries of my past friend and ask if he has any news of her whereabouts.

"Tell me, do you have any news of where Miss Ophelia is living and if she is well? She was very kind to me and I shall always be grateful for that. Was she a special friend of yours?"

He looks bemused by my questions, as I watch him push the small boxes back in position.

"You perhaps did not know that we are related? My dear *maman* who sadly died more than ten years ago was a cousin to Reverend Cedric, so you see Ophelia is from the next generation, as I am, too. It was just a chance meeting last year when I was travelling through on my way back to London and I felt it my duty to call on them both. I too know the heartbreak of losing a mother and naturally felt a sympathy for the sweet girl. Let me think. We did receive a letter a while ago. I can tell you she wore her poor father down with her demands to study, but her winning drawings enabled her to secure a place at an art school in Birmingham where she now paints and hopes to illustrate children's books."

"Oh that's wonderful! She had such talent and I'm so glad her wishes have been fulfilled. Thank you for telling me, and thank you for showing me your wonderful dolls."

Lady Caroline can be heard laughing gently and I sense a deal has been made today. I feel bound to return into the main shop, but am held back as Jean-Claude seizes my right hand and raises it to his lips in such a tender way I feel all of a flutter.

"*A la prochaine!* We shall meet again, Florence."

Chapter 34
The Collection

A cab is waiting patiently out in the street as pre-arranged and we are soon on our return journey up the hill towards The Crescent. I am content to sit back and listen as Lady Caroline enthuses about her new purchase, but we have no package with us. She has insisted upon a different layette, saying she would prefer its clothing to be white and not pale blue as had been shown. It will be delivered to her within a couple of weeks.

"And now you can understand my passion for collecting! Such perfection, although I rather think I shall be swayed by the German styles rather than the French Jumeau dolls. What do you think, Florence?"

I think I am floating on a cloud of dreams as I relive that emotional encounter, but I can't mention that. Instead I find myself chattering uncontrollably as I try to put all thoughts of Jean-Claude out of my mind.

"I've never seen anything like that before. They do not seem suitable toys for children to play with. I would be scared to even hold one. Once when he was younger my brother Thomas flew into a rage and he snatched one of my sister's ragdolls and threw it against the door. It ripped as it caught on a hook. Now if that had been one with a fine china head I'm sure it would have been broken in pieces, M'Lady."

I think I've said too much and feel relieved that we are nearing the house. Lady Caroline has the last words as we draw to a halt.

"We all have a need to collect fine items, Florence. I expect one day you too will have the desire to buy some ornament that you will proudly display in your own home. No doubt you'll recall the Chinese vases that are at Branswick Hall? One of my husband's ancestors had a passion for buying those. Then there's my sister Maud, who turns her nose up at anything that we may deem beautiful and chooses to collect what she calls modern works of art. To me, they are crude paintings where the artist simply daubs on a canvas. Simply ghastly, but then that's part of her mission in life to shock everyone. I shall have my adorable dolls to give me pleasure! I will now retire to my rooms, Florence, after a successful morning's visit."

I usually spend my free time in the summer evenings out on the cliff top, but today I still feel in such a dither. I have retreated to my room, pulled off my outer clothes and am laid prone on my bed still in my undergarments. It is often a relief to do this after I have relished taking a cold wash at my basin. My window is wide open in an attempt to capture any cooling breeze, so lying there, I relive this morning's unexpected encounter and break out in goose bumps just thinking about the handsome Jean-Claude. It scares me somewhat to feel my body quivering as my hands aimlessly fondle my swelling breast and then smooth their way towards my private regions. That very action shocks me and I sit bolt upright, ashamed of the thoughts forming in my head. Is this what it feels like to experience the first pangs of love?

I begin to understand why my sister Sue would talk at night in the darkness of our attic room, regaling us with George's amorous advances and of such unimaginable deeds that we would dismiss them as fanciful daydreams. Now I have those similar feelings and hope with all my heart that there will be other opportunities for us to meet and become more acquainted. With even more fanciful thoughts racing around my mind, I resolve to push them to one side and force myself to rise and hastily dress.

A sturdy work apron is vital so I can concentrate on a task I've been postponing. In the corner of my bedroom there is a small carton and I've yet to see what lies inside beneath the cloths and old newspaper wrappings. I'm in for a pleasant surprise as I unwrap the first parcel. It's a delicate porcelain shoe covered in dust, but I can make out that it has beautiful decorations of golden paint.

I shall enjoy this task, but the need for warm soapy water takes me downstairs to the laundry rooms. This is new territory for me to explore as I descend to the lower floor. I had hoped to find it empty this afternoon, but a laundry maid is still scrubbing the woodwork over by the deep sink.

"Beg pardon, Miss, I'm just finishing. Were you looking for somebody?"

She looks agitated, so I smile at her as I place the carton on a side bench.

"I'd be grateful if you could get me some warm soapy water. Lady Caroline has requested I see to the cleaning of these precious ornaments. Would you like to see one of them?"

The poor girl shrinks back at my invitation and looks terrified.

"No, I mustn't touch nought! Them's me instructions. I'd lose me job, Miss!"

"I just thought you might like to see the treasures in the box. Even I don't know what is hidden here!"

She moves to fill a kettle that is now heating up, and from a tall shelf I am presented with a stone jar.

"It's the flakes, Miss; you said you wanted soaps."

I start to unravel the first shoe and hear her gasp!

"Them's dead expensive! Cor, ain't they grubby!"

I find myself chuckling at her quaint expressions, but the question I now ask aloud is how I'm to clean between the fancy curves of the design. I hadn't anticipated this problem.

"I don't suppose you know where there are any fine brushes I could use."

In hindsight I suppose this was a rather foolish thing for me to say, but to my surprise I see her nodding.

"I knows where they keeps brushes. I snooped once and saw 'em in a drawer."

She flies out of the room and I stand listening to the kettle as it judders on the hot plate of the boiler. I'm just moving it to one side when she returns holding what I know to be pastry brushes. Oh dear, Mrs Heath will surely have a shock if she ever finds out what they are to be used for!

"Thank you, but I think it best we say nothing of this to anyone, do you understand?"

She nods and then disappears in a flash, terrified her actions will be found out.

I'm so reminded of the way I first felt when I started at Branswick Hall, being scared of putting a foot wrong. All that seems a lifetime ago. Now I can pride myself on achieving this trusted position. All thoughts of Jean-Claude evaporate as I begin to sort the contents.

Chapter 35
Cliff Tops

When I think about the simple life I left behind in the countryside, there is no comparison to the vibrancy I now see around me, as the town bustles with visitors all eager to be free from the grime of city living. August has brought its fair share of warm weather, but there is usually a refreshing breeze that comes off the sea and is most welcome. However, I have a certain amount of regret that overrides any pleasure I gain from living here. I had been waiting patiently in expectation of seeing Jean-Claude as I imagined he would be delivering the precious box to M'Lady, but when it had eventually arrived it was delivered by an elderly carrier and I had to come to terms with a feeling of resignation that any thoughts of us meeting again was merely a foolish fancy.

Now in my spare time I am more than content to explore further down the cliffs where I can observe people paddling as the waves tumble on to the shore. Some try to hitch up their long dresses and I start to wonder why we have to wear such long garments. I certainly would not be brave enough to attempt getting that close to the water's edge, but it is refreshing to watch the young girls who shamelessly tuck their shortened skirts into little bloomers and take great delight as the small waves break over their bare feet. Small boys are even braver, but often emerge with wet clothing as they dare themselves to go even deeper into the sea. Further down there is often an excitable queue waiting to use the newly installed lift. I am continually fascinated by the reactions on people's faces as they wait their turn to ride down the cliffs. They, like me are intrigued by this ingenious system that has been installed to enable access to the lower path by the sands. Some look terrified, others agog for the novel experience as they peer beneath to observe the water chambers. I have the urge to use it myself, but have to admit the thought of the motion still scares me. Perhaps if I were to be accompanied, I should feel brave enough to have a go. One small boy in the queue is trying to pull away from his father, calling out in terror.

"No, Papa! No! I'm frightened!"

He breaks free from his father's grasp and hurtles straight towards me in sheer panic, buffeting my legs and then falling to the ground where he lies, sobbing and upset. I feel rather sad for the little fellow and wonder if he will be scolded for such behaviour, so it is comforting to see his mother hasten over and scoop him into her arms, calming him with soothing words.

As I turn to walk away, the crowd settles down. I am thankful to see the distraught boy being led away with his family in a kindly manner.

It continually amazes me to see so many folk out walking each day, and I sometimes meet a few of Her Ladyship's acquaintances who will now nod a greeting as they recognise me in passing, and that is particularly pleasing to me. There is so much I want to tell Ma and my family of the daily happenings, but that would mean having to write every day, which is impossible. I shall store these tales in my head for when we meet again, but I cannot foresee that happening for quite some time. An empty seat further on beckons me to sit and I relish the feel of the warmth of the sun upon my face. My eyes close and I feel as if I'm in heaven!

"Florence?"

I just know that when I open my eyes that I shall recognise that familiar voice but am afraid of the consequences, so I sit there with them tightly shut. I sense a movement alongside me as an arm rests near to mine. It's Jean-Claude, I just know it is, and my suspicions are confirmed as I turn to face him. My dreams have been answered. He is not wearing his spectacles and looks at me with intense, deep brown eyes.

"This is truly *un plaisir* to meet again and I'm hoping is not giving you offence?"

His manner of speech amuses me with its lyrical way of mixing the two languages.

"I see from the glow of your bronzed face that you have already taken your walk, or I would suggest we stroll together. Perhaps another day?"

I address him as calmly as I can in an attempt to disguise my true emotions.

"How very nice to meet you again, Monsieur. Such a lovely day, you must be delighted to be in the fresh air rather than be working in the heat of your shop."

I hope I'm not being too forward with my words, but am flattered to have his attentions again.

"Much of my time I spend travelling; we have to make contacts with many stores around England so I am not always working here in Folkestone. There will come a day when I expect to inherit from my father, but that will not be for a while, God willing. But enough of this talk of work. Today I have a freedom as our shop is closed for a few days for repairs, so I came this way in case there should be a chance meeting with a familiar face!"

This has set me all of a quiver and I'm taken aback as he leans over and strokes the back of my left hand.

"I still have two days to enjoy this lovely weather before I next sail to France on business. Maybe you have some free time tomorrow when I can escort you to visit other sights in this busy town? If you wish, you can come with a friend and I will chaperone you both!"

His charm has already won me over, although he'll have no idea that I do not possess any friends and that will remain my secret. I feel bold enough to go along with his plans and rashly exclaim,

"How very kind of you, Monsieur. Unfortunately, I am needed tomorrow for M'Lady, but I will be free the following day from about two o'clock."

There, I've committed myself and there's no going back, so it is even more heart-warming to hear his response.

"My dear Florence, please to call me Jean-Claude, for I feel we are already friends! I shall be waiting for you then at the appointed time."

He stands to attention, bows slightly with his hand placed across his heart, then whispers "Au revoir" before walking off.

On my return to the house I am met by Mrs Heath, who has just been discussing menus with Her Ladyship. She looks me up and down and nods.

"My, you're looking bonny today; all this fresh air is giving you a healthy glow, or is there some other reason you look so happy?"

Now I'm in a quandary for I think she has guessed the true reason for my euphoric state. I try not to appear flustered so proudly hold my head up high as I reply, hoping to disguise my agitated self.

"It's such bliss to be here, Mrs Heath, I feel alive. I think I now understand the joy people get in living so near to the sea. I don't think I'd ever want to live anywhere else!"

There's an awkward pause as I finish speaking when I half expect the wrath of God to strike me down for telling such lies. What is happening to me? It's as if I am being swept along on a tidal wave out into deep waters where I have no control. Her comments bring me back to the present moment.

"Well, don't get too fond of us here. From what Her Ladyship has just intimated, you may soon be up and travelling again. Now, best you attend her upstairs, but tidy yourself up a bit lass. The wind has been playing catch with your lovely hair!"

Standing in front of my mirror I feel thoroughly ashamed of the way I spoke out downstairs. Then in a fit of anger I grab the hairbrush and release my coiled hair in order to scrape vigorously through the tangles until it hurts with each brushstroke. I imagine this is how a penitent feels when they chastise themselves and make myself stop, as tears roll uncontrollably down my face. I'm not one for being a great believer but I can't help myself from saying, "Please help me, God."

Chapter 36
Jean-Claude

The day has arrived when I am due to meet Jean-Claude and it both excites yet terrifies me in equal measure. I had felt on edge all morning in anticipation of seeing him again and ended up breaking one of her Ladyship's china dishes in my haste to be finished in good time. Thankfully, she said it was of no consequence, which greatly relieved me. I was undecided as to what I should wear, having first discarded a blue summer dress, and then my grey skirt and frilly blouse in favour of my work clothes. I thought they would be more appropriate for this first occasion. Although I still possess a couple of Ophelia's dresses, I considered it best to avoid wearing those, for I'm sure Jean-Claude would recognise their provenance. I still feel unsettled with my choice but am eagerly watching the hands on the clock by my bedside as it ticks towards the designated hour.

Meanwhile, Jean-Claude is feeling very pleased with himself today as he picks up a clothes brush and runs it over a dark blue velvet jacket hanging on the door. He aims to look dapper when he goes out, every bit the elegant man around town. He hopes that his father will finally be satisfied to think his son is escorting a young lady this afternoon. He feels he has to prove his worth and appease his father's demands to find a decent female companion. So, he sees this as a worthwhile exercise even though his true feelings are kept for certain secretive liaisons. In some ways, Jean-Claude is rather glad he made this approach to Florence, for he sees her as a naïve girl who should prove fun for a short while. He is convinced she will insist upon the company of another maid, and that will make him appear a most respectable host as they all walk out together. Eager to be on time, he walks briskly up to the cliff top.

As the hall clock strikes two, I purposely wait an extra five minutes, nervously hugging the cream shawl I have added in anticipation of any chilly breeze from the cliff top. Then, taking a deep breath, I open the front door and walk down the steps to meet him. It pleases me to see Jean-Claude smiling as he waits a few paces away. He nods his head in a military fashion to greet me, half whispering my name. He looks very handsome and I observe he is wearing spectacles today. They give him an air of authority but I am very aware that his eyes are critically scanning me from head to toe and the smile has changed to one of uncertainty. Now I feel ashamed of what I'm wearing and begin to regret my decision, but I am reassured as he speaks to me.

"You are alone, I see? Well, I am so very much looking forward to being in your company today, Florence. You look *tres charmant*. How very wise to add your shawl, as the sun is continually hiding behind the billowing clouds, but I do not think it will rain today. So, if you are agreeable, I thought we would take the pathway that winds to the bottom near the beach. It is quite easy that way."

Buoyed by his lyrical tone of voice, my confidence is boosted as I timidly reply, "Thank you. You are very kind."

His smile returns as we walk together across the swathe of grass at the front of the buildings, but even now I am contemplating the route he has suggested, for I know it will involve some steep parts, especially for the climb back later in the day. As we descend, he is keen to point out various landmarks and types of fishing boat that are leaving the harbour that afternoon. I am more occupied with making sure I don't fall and call out, "I haven't taken any of these paths before as they look quite steep and I'm a little scared it will make me feel dizzy." Hesitating as the path twists to the right, I hold my breath for a few seconds. This proves an opportune moment for Jean-Claude to proffer his arm as support and I feel thrilled!

"Dear Florence, you will be perfectly safe with me! We shall walk together! And do call me Jean-Claude, then it will be like we are a brother and sister."

At this suggestion I grin and gratefully accept the outstretched arm. The feel of his body so close to mine stirs a strange emotion, yet it also gives me an air of confidence and security as I cling tight. The paths dip and curve through pine walks and past scented bushes I do not recognise and sometimes we need to duck beneath low hanging branches from the windswept trees. It is with some relief when we meet other walkers on the reverse route who are glad to pause for a breath before they continue. Two sporty looking ladies are standing at one bend in the path, fanning themselves with their hands and feeling obliged to explain their situation.

"Do excuse our flustered appearance. We usually try to run up this last little section and I beat my sister again today!"

Jean-Claude is gallant and congratulates them. "Your devotion to exercise is very commendable, ladies!"

I am amused by their antics and the polite way in which he speaks. Finally, I can feel myself relaxing and I start to enjoy this little outing, even more so as we approach the lower paths, for the trees suddenly part and reveal the most vivid of sea views. This is so exciting and new to me I can't help but cry out,

"Oh look! We are getting so close and I can hear the waves!"

Now at the very base of the cliff I retract my arm and stand there quite speechless, having never seen a beach before.

"Welcome to our famous sands! As a young boy I would spend many hours building castles and deep moats."

I am quite overcome with the unexpected sight, for it looks as if the golden sands stretch for miles.

"It looks so small when you see it from up on the cliffs. I've never seen sand before. There is so much! But won't the sea wash it away every day?"

Jean-Claude holds out his hand. "No, they might shift around but they are always here. Come, let's stroll along and see if we can find any treasure."

This is the moment I have been dreaming of and I reach out to clasp his hand, thoroughly convinced he is showing his affection. Stepping onto the sands is a strange experience but immediately I feel unsteady as it moves beneath me. It's such a weird sensation feeling my little boots sinking as I attempt to walk. I only take a few steps and quickly decide it is most unpleasant. With a firm shake of my head I decline to carry on. "No, I don't feel safe! Please take me to the pathway!"

At this point Jean-Claude looks distinctly disappointed, and I can sense all his plans have been foiled, but he reluctantly leads me to the firm path before returning to the sands. Now he seems lost in thought, like a small boy on a mission, his eyes scanning for the odd shell or smoothed glass pebble as he trudges along the beach. It seems I am forgotten, left to my own devices as I stand alone on the path, so I begin to walk alone, all the while keeping my eye on Jean -Claude. He has moved further down the beach, occasionally stooping to retrieve a treasure and is too far away for me to converse with him. I now realise how foolish I have been in thinking this would turn out to be a perfect afternoon. I chided myself for earlier saying that I would never want to live anywhere else. At that moment the tempting images of the country lanes I know so well come flooding into my mind, along with memories of my family and I feel a certain shame at my dishonesty. All I can think of now is a way of ending this ordeal and returning to the clifftop at the earliest opportunity.

It seems my thoughts are answered as I spy a suitable path just ahead. Determined not to show any disappointment, I look back across the sands to where he seems to be chatting to some children who are playing near the water's edge. I force myself to call out in a loud voice.

"Jean-Claude, is this the path we need to take?"

He strides back, gesticulating with his hands and crying "No! No!" before joining me on the firm pathway. I am totally bemused for he chats as if nothing untoward has happened between us.

"Oh, but I have a treat in store for you! Just a little further along. We shall walk together!"

Jean-Claude grips my elbow and propels me forward, all the while offering profuse apologies for leaving me on my own.

"Forgive me, I sometimes lose all track of time when I am down on the beach. Now I want this to be a special treat, *mon petite chou fleur*, especially for you!"

He leans close and I feel confused with all these mixed messages but it is so easy to respond to his alluring murmurs.

"You tease me Jean-Claude! So, what is this treat you talk of?"

We are nearing a handsome brick cottage that takes pride of place overlooking the beach. It is hard to imagine who might live here but I assume it belongs to someone very wealthy for it looks most picturesque.

To my surprise, Jean-Claude leads the way up the white steps to a half open door and I fully anticipate I am to be introduced to its esteemed residents. I get a shock when I see what is inside!

We did laugh about it much later, for it had been so unexpected to discover we were at the base of the newly installed cliff funicular railway. I was captivated by the thought of using it and clung to Jean-Claude with bated breath as we entered. As the lift began to rise and the wide vista of the sea came into view, I was won over by the whole experience and didn't want the ride to end. Jean-Claude was clearly pleased that his efforts had been appreciated and I was grateful to be spared the arduous climb back. I did not object and it seemed quite natural when he casually stretched his arm around my waist as we walked the final few yards.

"I want there to be other occasions when we walk out, dear Florence. Do say that will be to your liking?"

I am so overcome with happiness I do not object but welcome this advance, for it seems to indicate my earlier fears of rejection are groundless. I think long and hard about what to say.

"This has all been very pleasant. Thank you so much, Jean-Claude. I shan't ever forget how special the lift ride was this afternoon. And now I must bid you *au revoir*. Thank you once again."

Before I make a fool of myself I turn and run up the steps with my heart beating fast as I remember the closeness of his body to mine. I catch him waving to me then watch from the open door as he quickly heads for the town with renewed purpose.

Chapter 37
Letters

The events of that day gave me much to think about and I was left feeling very unsure of myself, to the point at which I realised what a complete fool I had been to think he actually had feelings for me. I had behaved in an unseemly fashion in allowing my impulsive nature to take hold. Consequently, I vowed to dismiss any further thoughts of contact with Jean-Claude. My duties now would be solely for Her Ladyship and I aimed to work even harder and thus prove myself worthy of my post. The daily routine is certainly not arduous and I seem more at ease these days as she trusts me to help her dress and talks to me as if we were close friends.

"I want you to come with me today, Florence, but we will not be walking!"

She likes to pause and leave these hints up in the air so that I'm not sure if a response is merited. This morning I am watching at her mirror as she tries to apply the new face creams herself to cover her blemished skin.

"You are doing very well, M'Lady. Perhaps a little gentle rubbing to soften the edges?"

I lean over and blend one of the edges.

"There! No one would ever know! May I pin your hair now, or are you planning to wear a hat this afternoon?"

I hope this might entice her to reveal her plans, but she seems intent on keeping me in suspense a little longer.

"I shall be wearing my hat Florence, so can we say "man the ropes"?"

This is our little joke. I know exactly what she means. It involves much plaiting and coiling, but it's a style that fits tidily

176

beneath any type of hat she chooses to wear. Do I see her grinning or is it just a friendly smile as she looks back through the mirror?

"I shall require my long coat today and I suggest you also wear a warm jacket as the September air can be much cooler."

Her statement intrigues me for I still consider it to be a warm day. Indeed, we have yet to light any fires in the house. Perhaps Lady Caroline is thinking of us taking the evening air instead? As I finish my task she looks extremely satisfied with my efforts and turns to say,

"Two o'clock as usual? Thank you, Florence. And now I must go down for one of my good friends is due to call this morning. Would you tidy this before you leave?"

I always think it most civil of Her Ladyship to ask these tasks of me rather than giving an order that you feel bound to obey. Yes, I consider myself very lucky indeed to be here, to be accepted among fine company and be afforded these little treats when we go out together.

The reason for wearing a warm coat becomes obvious when we arrive on the lower road by the sea and dismount from the hired cab. Lady Caroline has brought me to explore the elegant Victoria Pier and we are now standing at its imposing iron gateway as it guards the entrance. I'm not sure what to expect for the metalwork reminds me of animal cages that I've seen illustrated in old newspapers. I get the impression that once we have gone through the twisting barriers there will be no return and I find this slightly unnerving. I see her proffering money and then she turns a bar and is through to the other side.

"How easy is that! Just push it firmly, Florence. It won't bite you!"

She is laughing at my timidity and I guess for her this is not a new experience.

The way the bar suddenly flies open makes me jump but I hurry through half afraid it will spring back and hit me.

"Bravo! Welcome to the pier! Oh, I know it's my incorrigible behaviour, but it always amuses me to bring my friends here and watch their reactions as we enter! Now we can take our stroll and view the world from the other side."

And so we walk together and I feel proud to be doing so as the word 'friend' floats around in my head. To be treated as one of her friends is indeed quite an honour and makes me very proud to be with her. We tread the wooden boards and peer over the sides at the people below, some strolling, some sitting and others happily digging into the sand to amuse their families. From this height they appear so small, then I notice the further we walk that we are now directly above the sea. I immediately feel uncomfortable, especially when we come across thin gaps between the planks where you can see the waves below. I pause and she looks concerned, one hand now steadying her hat that wavers in the breeze.

"The wind usually gets stronger towards the end, but if we go further on you'll be able to see the Grand Pavilion. I have attended several times to witness the successful artistes who have performed here."

"Are you sure it is safe to walk any further, M'Lady? I find this a little unsettling for fear we may fall through!"

"Perfectly safe, I assure you. This has been a welcome addition to our lovely town attracting visitors who come for its spectacular views. We'll just go a little further on. Stop! Now I want you to turn around and look back!"

I now understand about seeing a different world. Lady Caroline looks lost in thought as she gazes at the shoreline.

"The whole effect is meant to give one an impression of being afloat at sea and don't you agree it looks simply splendid with the high cliffs one side and the harbour walls to our left? I love to stand here in all kinds of weather and imagine I am miles away on the wide seas!"

I am finding it overwhelming, for the panorama before me is one of the most impressive things I've ever seen. Just seeing how small everything looks from a distance is quite a novel experience. Even the tall grand houses I've come to know resemble little boxes perched high on the cliff top and the gathering clouds look as if they are about to knock them over. I cannot thank her enough for allowing me to have accompanied her today. It is just unfortunate that an unexpected fall of light rain has forced us to hurry back for I swear I could have spent longer being captivated by the whole scene.

To add to my pleasure, we take a circular tour for the return journey so that I get a glimpse of the fishing harbour, but all I see are masts lying at precarious angles that look most unsafe. She is patient to explain how the tides affect the moored ships and I am ashamed I know so little about the different aspects of living by the sea. As we pass through the town, Lady Caroline indicates other grand buildings, some still under construction.

"Folkestone is a popular resort for London visitors, hence the need to build even grander hotels. One can never be bored living here, Florence, but it pains me to think I shall shortly be leaving it all."

I am rather startled, not so much by what she says, but the fact she takes my hand in hers.

"Nothing lasts forever and I shall shortly be needed back at Branswick Hall. I do so want you to return with me, Florence, for you have made me feel human again."

Nothing has prepared me for this upheaval, although looking back I now see that the whole year has been one of rapid changes for me when I have been thrust from one situation to another. The euphoria of the day gives way to a feeling of sadness, for I know I shall miss this place and all the happy times it has given me. I am unsure how to respond and as she continues to enlighten me.

"Today I have received a letter from my husband. He wishes me to be present when he entertains some dear friends that we both know. I will go with a heavy heart, but feel it my duty on this occasion. I do so hate being away from the sea."

She settles back in the cab and there is an uncomfortable silence save for the regular sound of hoof beats as we are drawn along.

"I will discuss arrangements with you later as I dress for dinner. A very pleasant outing, don't you agree?"

What I find so enjoyable about my current post is having time to myself. I have much to think about with the prospect of travelling back to the Hall, but am grateful that I shall still be expected to assist Her Ladyship. On entering the house, I am handed a small brown envelope, so am free to escape to my room to savour the contents. I know from the writing it has come from Lizzie and that pleases me. If I am to return with Lady Caroline the prospect of meeting the family once more lightens my mood. I read it slowly to digest the words but they are brief and to the point. It worries me to discover that Ma is still unwell, but is refusing to let any of her children send for a doctor. Lizzie writes of her being in great pain and sounds most concerned, so she is begging me to seek leave to return as soon as possible. I feel shocked, but find it so ironic having just been informed that we shall shortly be leaving the coast.

I hasten to find paper and a pencil to send a reassuring reply to Lizzie that I shall be back quite soon. It pleases me to think I shall be seeing them and I shall have so many tales to tell about my experiences both in London and here in Kent that I hope will thrill them all.

Chapter 38
The Town

Word has reached the staff that our departure is scheduled for the end of the month, on the Wednesday before Michaelmas Day. I am aware that they will be retained as Lady Maud is shortly due to return. However, I shall miss the company of Mrs Heath who has been very kind to me. I know I shall have regrets at leaving this adorable place, but I am buoyed by the fact that I have been given permission to visit my father and Ma at home, for they will be celebrating a wedding anniversary on that very day. I am hoping that by then Ma will be feeling a little better in order to enjoy that special occasion. Lady Caroline spoke very frankly to me this morning and said it was my duty to visit and gave her approval. While I was helping to close the intricate buttons at the back of her lilac taffeta dress, she demanded that my presence be required all morning. I think I am getting used to the way she comes out with these tantalising statements, followed by a weighty pause that always leaves me in suspense!

"This morning I am expecting Madame Jacques to call and measure me for new dresses. I am tiring of all these heavy flounces and awkward fittings and wish to have a more simple design. She will be calling at half past eleven."

I'm not quite sure what my role will be, so I assume it is for assistance when M'Lady is being measured. This is all new to my experience, but I can't help but notice how her eyes are playfully laughing at me.

"What would you choose, Florence? What are your favourite colours?"

This requires some quick thinking as I think about Her Ladyship's height and colouring. Her hair is now flecked with silver tones and with her paler skin I think she would be better suited to stronger colours.

"It would be lovely if you wore something in deep blue or rich emerald, M'Lady. Please don't be offended at my suggestions."

The way she now looks at me with one hand suppressing her laughter, makes me feel I've made a fool of myself again. I am totally unprepared for her next outburst.

"But Florence, I am planning for you to have a new dress as well! It will be my gift to you for the kindness you have shown me! I'm asking what colours you would choose!"

And that is how we come to be standing in one of the sitting rooms below, with a warm fire to take away the morning's chill. I still can't believe this is happening and feel very excited and honoured. Contrary to my expectation, Madame Jacques is not of French descent, but a plain-speaking English woman with a brisk efficient manner. She has a young lady assisting her who shows many examples of fine fabrics along with sketches of various designs. It doesn't take much persuasion for Lady Caroline to agree on a simple design adorned with elegant puffed sleeves that only requires two simple buttons at the wrist.

I like to think I may have influenced her choice of colour, for she does indeed select a rich deep blue velvet with a discreet cream lace trim. When my turn arrives I feel tongue tied and struggle to think clearly. I feel uncomfortable as Madame Jacques takes her measurements around my breasts and waist, but it is done swiftly and now I am confused as the swathes of material are displayed in front of me.

"I think you would suit something like this. It will complement your dark hair perfectly."

Lady Caroline is pointing towards a coral pink example and I feel the softness of the linen material and nod in agreement, thankful for her intervention. The meeting is concluded and the ladies depart with arrangements in place for the dresses to be ready within four days.

"I shall retire to my bedroom this afternoon, Florence. All this activity makes one quite tired!"

I smile because I can see from her grin that she is exaggerating again. She is more than happy to spend her time without any company.

Left to my own devices, I am determined to step out on the cliff tops in order to absorb the changing scene and fix it forever in my memory. I think a warm jacket might be suitable, but I'm still not sure why I scooped up my leather purse to pop into one of the pockets. I think my inner self is still curious to see what lies further down towards the town, so whilst I am tossing over the morning's events, I lose all track of time and then discover I have strayed further and am now facing a small parade of shops. They are not as grand as the establishment owned by Monsieur Leroc, but are neat and well presented. A tantalising aroma drifts from a baker's shop and I am captivated by the array of tiered wedding cakes on display in the window. I swiftly pass the next window with its interesting selection of spectacles, but find myself drawn towards the third window where there are boxes of expensive items of jewellery. Wistfully I look around, but it becomes very evident that the meagre amount of money I carry with me will in no way permit me to purchase even the smallest of brooches. So sadly I must dream of a future day when I can fulfil my wish to give Ma some pearls. I am just about to leave when a tall, well-dressed gentleman appears beside me, scanning the objects on show and it is then I suddenly feel very vulnerable knowing I have strayed alone into this unknown part of the town. The fact he smells strongly of drink alarms me.

"Pretty trinkets for a very pretty young lady? And all on your own? Now what takes your fancy?"

The way he is leering at me causes my heart to beat rapidly and I blurt out the first thing that comes into my head. "I'm on my way to meet my brother."

My only thoughts are to flee in the hopes of finding other people in the area with whom I could feign a conversation and thus avoid any further confrontation. In my confusion I step away, now unsure of the route I need to take for my return to the Crescent. I walk as briskly as I can, but am conscious of his footsteps following behind me and then panic starts to set in. I find myself desperate for help so take a sudden left turn, which leads me into a street I vaguely recognise and then I feel so thankful, for it seems my prayers have been answered.

Jean-Claude is ahead of me, talking animatedly to a young man. The sheer relief at seeing a familiar face forces me to bravely call out his name in order to attract his attention. I hasten towards him, still aware I am being followed, but eager to be by his side. Jean-Claude looks distinctly surprised to see me, but takes my hands in a welcoming gesture. I speak quickly and in low tones. "Help me! I'm being followed."

Both he and his friend are on alert as they look around. They can't fail to see the lone figure now walking straight past us, his eyes fixed to the ground as if in denial. We stand in silence until the footsteps have faded away.

"You can breathe easy, for that unsavoury cad has disappeared from sight. *Ma chère,* Florence! Now I beg to know what brings you here unaccompanied."

His friend is waiting impatiently, fidgeting with a kerchief in his top pocket and looking somewhat annoyed at my sudden intrusion to their conversation. Jean-Claude makes a swift introduction and explains that I am an old friend. He seems to be making excuses to the young man, stressing the importance of immediately escorting me home, but I can see this is not met with approval for his friend pouts in a childlike manner. I feel the need to apologise for interrupting their conversation but the opportunity is lost as he curtly bows and speaks plainly to Jean-Claude.

"I trust we can resume this meeting tomorrow? I shall demand a full explanation."

We part company as he strides away, clearly annoyed at my intrusion and demands upon Jean-Claude, but I am spared any further guilt as I am firmly led back towards the road that heads for the cliff tops. It feels good to be walking alongside this good-looking man and to have his undivided attention. It is such a relief to feel safe that I find myself unable to stop talking. In describing the recent unsavoury event I tell him everything, the reasons for my lingering at the shop window and regret that I was unable to afford a small gift to take home to Ma. I thank him profusely for being there to help me, but feel bound to inform him that my time in Folkestone is coming to an end. That fact saddens me knowing how much I shall miss his kind ways. He listens patiently, nodding his head and waiting for me to quieten down. When we finally reach the open levels that overlook the sea, I have regained my composure and thank him once more.

"I feel safe now, but appreciate that you have escorted me home. I must bid you goodbye."

There is nothing I can add to that except to wonder if things might have been different for us both if my stay had been longer. Jean-Claude straightens his spectacles and then smiles affectionately.

"But you will be back, I'm sure of that. The sea has a way of calling you and we are held under its magic spell! So I will say *au revoir* and you will understand why!"

When I reach the steps to the house I look back and watch him disappear as he hurries down the sloping street and out of my life. Suddenly the appeal of close family and my past friends is paramount as I now contemplate my future.

Chapter 39
Final Days

Lady Caroline makes it her mission to fill her last days by inviting the many friends she has acquired in the area to dine with her. When I take a meal with Mrs Heath I hear all about the sumptuous food she has to order. It all seems very lavish, but I should not complain for we get to taste many examples of chef's finest recipes. In the three months I have been here I have yet to encounter this famous chef Phillipe. I'm told he rarely leaves his kitchen and only allows one trusted hand to work with him. I know I shall miss the wonderful food that he also provides for the staff for it is far superior to anything I've eaten before.

My presence has been required for many extra tasks so I have little free time, but am more than happy to be occupied. This will be our last night here so one travelling chest is already packed for travel and now I'm required to help Lady Caroline choose which dress she is to wear this evening. I've gained a great deal of enjoyment from helping M'Lady on these occasions. She is particularly thrilled when the newly made dress arrives as promised and this is her choice tonight. I am asked to create a hairstyle that will complement the soft drapes so I suggest she let her hair fall loose, as it has such a natural curl. The resulting image is that of a much younger woman and she is delighted with the total effect.

"You made a good choice with this rich colour, Florence. I trust that you like your own dress as much as I like this?"

I must think carefully about my answer for I do not want to offend. It is indeed a work of art, but far too grand for me. It is still hanging in full view from my bed where I look at it in awe, but I struggle to think how I will ever have an opportunity to wear it.

"Your Ladyship has been most generous and it is a beautiful dress that I shall be proud to wear. I am very grateful to you."

Maybe the art of telling these little white lies is becoming a habit and that does trouble me. However, I have no time to ponder further on this dilemma as I fasten a silver pendant around her neck and compliment her on her appearance.

"Very satisfactory, M'Lady, and I'm sure your guests will agree."

With a happy smile she sweeps gracefully towards the door. I feel it my duty to add, "I hope you have a very pleasant evening."

She pauses, and looks back to where I am still standing.

"I do not enjoy the prospect of staying at Branswick, but it will only be for a short while, Florence, and we shall return. Yes, we shall return! Tonight, I aim to forget all that and enjoy myself."

There is a quiet satisfaction in knowing I have done well and have been appreciated, but I am happy to escape to my bedroom where I have time to reflect. As I look longingly out of my window at the darkening skies, I want to capture every last moment I am living here. It feels as if I am being torn in two for one half of me has been so content here in Folkestone, yet the pull of reuniting with my dear family is just as strong. What scares me most is the daunting prospect of meeting again with the superior Mrs Baynton. She has always filled me with fear and I'm convinced she will still be as scathing about my work. As for encountering His Lordship I shall be on my guard. With all the facts I have been privy to about his relationship with his wife, I do not know how I shall react towards him.

Lights have appeared out at sea as several fishing boats head for deeper waters and I find that most soothing to watch as I clear my mind. Tonight it is calm and still, and that makes me happy for the brave men who venture out for their catch. I realise how much I am going to miss living here and sigh as I look up at the black night sky. High above one solitary star seems to shimmer so brightly as if to say, "I'll still be here when you return!"

All that remains for me to do is to work out how best to stow my beautiful pink dress and other belongings into my travel bag whilst I wait upon the call to attend Her Ladyship as she retires later this evening. There's a bubble of excitement growing in me! I am going home!

It is a tedious journey as we travel back to London by steam train, but I am kept amused by the silly guessing games that Lady Caroline invents to pass the time. As we sit on opposite seats she can see ahead and will tease me by calling out little clues. The latest one is, "I see something that is brown!"

This will conjure up an image of a wooden gate, or a cow or even a bare tree, but my guesses are rarely correct. On this occasion when the brown object comes into my view, it turns out to be pile of steaming dung. Then she just bursts out laughing and I am thankful we have the compartment to ourselves to spare any blushes from fellow passengers.

Mrs Heath had pressed a small basket into my hands, so we are able to sustain ourselves with her tasty bread and meat fillings. I decline to have any drink for obvious reasons as with each passing mile I became more agitated. In addition to the food, Mrs Heath had handed over a surprise package that had been urgently delivered that morning addressed to me. Although I am curious as to the contents, I pledge to pack it safely and open it when our journey is done.

We have to transfer by hansom cab to yet another station and this has been efficiently arranged by none other than the trusted footman who must have travelled elsewhere on the train. I did finally discover that this is the mysterious Levison, a quiet man who will not be drawn into any conversation. It does not please me to be amongst the throng of London traffic with the overbearing smells and noises that seem to come from every direction and Lady Caroline begins to look weary and more downhearted with every moment that passes. I try making light-hearted conversation to cheer her but to no effect, so it is with relief we board the next train for the final stretch of our journey. I watch as she closes her eyes and sleeps and before long, I too am dozing, soothed by the rhythmic sound as the wheels pass over the tracks.

Our ultimate arrival at Branswick Hall is greeted in a formal manner as staff are lined up to cordially receive Lady Gressingham. His Lordship appears all smiles as he presses his lips upon her gloved hand. But that is all I get to see for I am speedily ushered in an ungainly fashion by a junior footman towards a rear entrance where I recall only deliveries are usually made. This is quite disconcerting after the freedoms I have been used to and I feel indignant that I am being treated this way. Nothing is said, but I am shown into a small store room where I am confronted by the unexpected sight of my two brothers, Henry and Joe standing there. The brief thrill I experience on seeing them swiftly evaporates as I observe the black armbands they wear. I feel my heart sinking and there is an awkward silence as our eyes lock.

"She was buried today and you weren't there! You should have come sooner! She kept asking for you and now it's too late."

Henry spits out the last words and turns his back on me, fighting back the tears. The sudden shock of his words makes me feel sick, so that my body starts to tremble and I think I'm going to collapse.

My younger brother Joe moves forward and steadies me and seems to realise I am struggling to know what this all means. He speaks quietly, but in a deeper voice that unsettles me with its maturity.

"It's Ma, Flo. She went all of a sudden. Doctor said it were a heart attack. None of us knew. You weren't to blame, though Henry has took it bad. He's blaming everyone, including Pa. Says he should have called the doctor sooner."

The shame I experience on hearing this shattering news engulfs me and I break down and sob into Joe's arms. My body is numb and it feels as if my whole world has crumbled from beneath me. I look up to his tear-stained face and can only whisper, "I'm sorry, Joe, I'm so sorry."

He holds me tight and waits patiently for my sobs to calm down, but I am further moved to tears on feeling Henry's comforting arms when he walks over to embrace us both. He appears full of remorse and murmurs his apologies.

"Oh Flo, I'm sorry, too. I didn't mean to have a go at you. We was all so looking forward to you coming back."

A discreet cough from outside the door serves as a signal for us to stand apart and I fully expect that I am being called away to attend Lady Caroline. However, a footman beckons for Henry to step outside into the passageway from where we hear a muffled conversation. He reappears to inform us that I am given special leave to return home and an open carriage will be made available to transport us on special orders from His Lordship.

"It's all been arranged, Flo. We need you back home."

He leads me like a blind child out into the courtyard where I almost stumble as I am helped up on to a seat. Joe and Henry sit beside as if to keep me safe. I note my belongings are already strapped on securely, but this final journey of a long and eventful day is going to be the least enjoyable as I face up to reality.

Chapter 40
Family

My first thoughts are to dash to the privy and relieve myself and there the unfamiliar smells set me heaving until I am physically sick. I wipe my mouth with a handkerchief hoping it will not be too obvious, but feel glad of the fresh air as I walk down the cinder path to confront my family. What strikes me is the eerie silence in the kitchen for there is no chatter or merry laughter, only the saddest of faces that breaks my heart to see. Mary is the first to move from her chair and she cuddles me with affection.

"You will stay, won't you, our Flo? I can't do it by myself."

Her pleading eyes only serve to remind me that I am needed now. There is no sign of Pa anywhere, but it is a pitiful sight, seeing my other siblings. I realise I am totally ignorant about their circumstances so my only instinct is to grab an apron. In the calmest voice I can summon without fear of offending I ask if they have eaten today. Young Jack stands up and holds out an empty tin.

"I just finished off the buns Ma made… I hope she don't mind."

I barely recognise him in the ill-fitting suit he wears. He looks apologetically at us and I realise how hard it must be for them to accept she has been just been laid to rest. I am still ignorant of all the facts and wonder why Lizzie has not come forward in her usual way to greet me. I had expected to see one or other of my older sisters taking charge and this puzzles me. There is no sign of Sue, but now I spot Lizzie who is huddled in one corner where the boys usually sleep. She is cradling sister Harriet in an attempt to stop her shaking. I fight back the tears not knowing what to do next, so it heartens me to hear Henry unexpectedly call out.

"Right, Jack, get scrubbing those spuds. Tom, stir yourself, lad; your hens will be missing you. Have you collected any eggs today? Thought not. Off you go. Mary, you sort out some vegetables. We need to eat and it will do us good to be busy."

With some semblance of daily routine, we go about these tasks in a mechanical fashion, the conversation stilted as I glean the truth about Ma's illness and the harrowing scene of as she was buried in the local churchyard. Strangely, it feels quite natural to be working once more in a kitchen for it gives me a focus, although it delays the opportunity to have a private talk with Lizzie. As I carve the remnants of a dried ham to supplement our meal, she comes over and kisses me on the cheek.

"Dearest Flo, so pleased to see you and so much to tell." She catches her breath and holds tight to the table's edge, her head hung low. "Oh Ma, what do we do now? I can't, I just can't…"

I stop and give her the warmest hug I can with reassuring words as I rub her arms as if to bring her back to life.

"Sh! Hush, Lizzie. I realise this has been a hard day for you all. Keep it for a bit longer and then when we've all eaten together you and I will find a quiet place to talk."

There is a calmness as we all appreciate the makeshift meal, but also a reluctance for people to speak out. So much has changed in such a short time with my own experiences now pushed firmly to the back of my mind. The shock of seeing Harriet in such a pitiful state of nerves is almost unbearable. She does not seem to recognise me and constantly rocks herself as she later crouches on her bed. However, it is good to learn that Joe is now in training as a coachman and has lodgings at the stables and Jack, too, has work. As for poor Thomas, I can foresee he will be lost without Ma there to coax and praise him. He sits there cutting his food into neat little sections before deciding which one to eat. I'm told that he has stopped speaking and just sits in his dream world, sorting and stacking an old pile of playing cards. Thankfully, Mary still has a habit of chattering about her school and friends and perhaps everyone needs to have a bit of normality today to alleviate the sadness. No one has mentioned Father so far and I'm almost afraid to ask, for it looks as if Henry has taken over his role. I shall have to be patient and wait until I talk with my sister.

Under the fading September sun and well wrapped in our coats, Lizzie and I walk along the lane, arms linked in our old familiar fashion as we head towards a dry stone wall we know well. Here we can sit and she can finally unburden herself. At first, she is eager to hear my stories about the seaside, but I am too ashamed to indulge in what now seem like fantasies and beg her to tell me everything. As she speaks, I can see it is like a release for her as she shares the stories with me and I get to understand what the family has been through. It's no surprise to finally learn that Pa is drinking heavily and consequently has lost his job.

"That was the final blow for Ma with no wages coming in and her hearing about him staying most nights over at the inn. There is even talk of another woman, so she and Henry barred him from coming back to the cottage. He did turn up at the graveside, but he was reeling around and we were so ashamed. It's been hard trying to manage with our combined money, but I don't like leaving Tom and Harriet when I have to work. She was treated so badly it's turned her mind. So full of bruises and cuts where she was beaten that Ma took pity on her, but we never let on about her losing the poor babby or Father would have turned her out. Now she gets scared at any callers for fear that brute Mason turns up again."

My other question is about our eldest sister Sue and her notable absence, only to be told she is now living at the farm and is set to marry George in the coming week. This sounds like good news, but Lizzie hesitates before continuing.

"You see, that's another scandal that shook Ma, "cos Sue deliberately got herself in the family way so she could marry

193

him. It all got too much for Ma to bear and we all thought it was the worry of everything that pained her so much. Do you know, I envied you, Flo, away from all this without a care in the world? It's been so hard and now with Ma gone I don't know how we shall cope."

In the uncomfortable silence that follows I recognise my only course of action is to be a dutiful daughter and thus with a heavy heart I vow to relinquish my current post. Something holds me back from saying this aloud to Lizzie, other than to placate her by saying, "We'll work something out, don't you worry."

She jumps down with a resigned air, brushing off the stray leaves from her coat. "We'd better be heading home, Flo. It's getting dark. Now you must tell me all about working with these posh people! I can't believe you got to see our capital city as well!"

I do so want to share my news, but cannot bring myself to do so just yet and so make the hasty excuse that I need to go to Ma's grave to say my goodbyes.

"Five minutes, I promise and I'll be back."

Our parting hug only serves to bring us close to tears once more as I turn towards the church and graveyard.

It doesn't seem logical to be on my knees talking to a newly dug mound of earth when I have no physical evidence of my mother lying there, but I feel the need to apologise for not coming home when she had need of me. One solitary wreath of paper flowers from the family has been placed in the centre, so as I had gathered a handful of wild red campion and stray dog roses on my way there, I proceed to lay them respectfully on either side. At one end is a small wooden cross that I'm sure must be Jack's handiwork, for it has her name neatly carved upon it. There is a poignant irony on seeing the words "Caroline Gibbs", for it conjures up recent memories of Her Ladyship and sets me crying again. I almost wish the darkness would swallow me up as I do not want to face the future. Then I hear a familiar soothing voice.

"Lizzie said you would be here. We're all so sorry about your poor mother going so sudden."

I know without a doubt that it is Albert speaking and just hearing him gives me a faint glimmer of hope that our friendship can be reignited. He is quick to offer a hand as I struggle to stand and that reassuring touch strengthens my resolve to stay. In the fading light I can still make out how tall he has grown and it is a joy to be looking at his kind face once more. He looks very distinguished with a full ginger beard, but I do wonder how much he has changed in my absence and whether this is just a polite encounter.

"Welcome home, Flo. I've missed you and your smiles and I know this is not the time to be talking of smiling, but there will be better days ahead. Come. Let me walk you home."

It seems quite natural for me to slip my arm through his and this comforting act is enough to settle me as we stroll back in silence. There is no need for us to talk for I sense Albert will wait patiently until I feel able to do so. As I glance up into the night sky there is one solitary star shining directly above us and it sets me wondering. Now I shall forever see it as a tribute to dear Ma, for it will be her special star and will shine wherever I am bound.

Chapter 41
Resignation

It took several attempts for me to write a letter explaining my current situation and that I felt obliged to leave my service with the Gressinghams. I suppose I was being cowardly for not presenting myself at the Hall to give my reasons in person, but I knew the mere sight of Her Ladyship would have such a hold on me and that would inevitably sway my decision. When I knew the next carrier was heading that way I asked him to deliver both letter and my uniform, which I neatly folded and packed inside a bag made from some of Ma's treasured linen. I thought long and hard about whether I should also return my own coral dress, but couldn't bear to part with it. I then had the worrying dilemma as to where it could be stored away from the prying eyes of my sisters, so it is now tightly rolled into a second bag and hidden at the back of our shared clothes cupboard. This secretive act seems to mark the end of my aspiration to better myself as I now have to focus solely on holding our family together.

There is an air of calm resignation as we all resume our daily activities, but my biggest concern is how we are going to be able to afford to stay in the cottage. Neighbours from Higher Weldon have been very supportive knowing our circumstances, offering help and bringing us food. Albert's mother Mrs Mason did kindly suggest I could make cakes that she could sell on her market stall. That would at least provide a further source of income so after some thought we agreed it would be more profitable if I concentrated on apple pies. There has been such a glut this season and I've seen the full baskets stored in an outside shed. I suspect that Albert himself may have been behind this move, but any suggestions are more than welcome at present.

I try to put all thoughts of the past few months out of my mind. The small package addressed to me still lays unopened in my travelling bag and I haven't the heart to reveal its contents. Any reminder of Mrs Heath and her kindness will only make me think longingly about living by the sea. Three weeks have now passed when we have all tried to establish new routines. I'm rather glad Mary is at school, especially as we've been told she now helps out with the younger ones. This will focus her mind, but I'm grateful she is still eager to assist with any jobs when she returns home. On days when I feel I can no longer cope, she will come bouncing in, full of chatter and it warms my heart to hear her. My initial fear that we would become destitute has disappeared, for with Jack now employed as a delivery lad, and with money coming from Lizzie and my two other brothers, we are managing to get by.

It is early in the afternoon and I am quietly sitting in the front parlour trying to repair one of Jack's torn shirts. I can see through the door where Thomas is at the kitchen table with Harriet. She is much calmer and to my surprise has taken it upon herself to sit with him and play cards. It has given her a purpose in life and he dotes on her as a substitute mother figure. In a rare moment she speaks out to him.

"Don't forget, Tom, you're the doorkeeper. Do you understand?"

Thomas is still refusing to communicate, but I can see he is thinking and Harriet looks thankful when he finally nods his head as if agreeing.

"Good lad, you'll be the best doorman in the world! Don't let any strangers in!"

It may be early days, but after our recent tragedy I feel grateful it has presented these two with an opportunity to be of help to each other. It also seems a favourable moment for me to thank her. I place the shirt to one side and choose my words carefully as I call out to her.

"I'm so glad you are here, Harriet. I couldn't manage without your help and Tom thinks the world of you. It's so sad our lives have been turned upside down, but the best plan now is that we all pull together. There will be better times ahead, I'm sure."

Harriet looks ashamed and hangs her head. She still hesitates to speak directly to me and I assume she also blames me for not being there when Ma was unwell. I find it quite touching how she rises from her chair and gives her brother a tender pat on his shoulders before joining me on the small settee.

The agitated manner in which she constantly wrings her hands together is an untimely reminder of Lady Louisa and I find myself praying that Harriet will find the strength to overcome her past. It takes me by surprise to see her pick up the torn shirt, inspect it and then steadily continue the repair I had started, but I am further stunned when she finally talks.

"You're the only one who never judged me, Flo, and I'm dead sorry you had to leave your job, but we couldn't have done it without you. Ma would have been real proud."

There is a joint realisation that things are better left unsaid as we sit each with our private thoughts, but I seize the moment with a sudden idea.

"I'd forgotten you were so good at sewing, Harriet. It's just a thought, but why don't we put word out in the town and village that you could do repairs, possibly make clothes for folk? Of course, not if you don't want to."

The suggestion has been made and for the first time I see a glimmer of confidence return as she reaches for more cotton thread.

We are all startled to hear a sudden rapping at the door, at which Tom hurtles towards it and pulls the bolt across.

"Go away! There's no one here!"

We have to smile at his funny ways, but I coax him to stand back. "Good work, Thomas. Now let me see who is calling."

I instantly recognise the carrier, who stands there looking slightly alarmed.

"Are you OK in there? Only I thought maybe there was something odd going on with all the shouting. Got a letter for you, orders to be hand delivered to the young lady in person. I see she's used the posh paper! Here you are then, and I bid you good day."

With that he doffs his cap and disappears round the cottage and we hear the cart being driven away. I stand there holding the envelope wary of its contents, but to see my name written there in such a grand manner pleases me. Tom is agitated and desperate for me to move, so I return to the parlour. He is intent on his new task of guarding the door by closing and reopening it several times until he feels confident for it to eventually click tight.

I'm almost afraid of opening the letter so place it by my side. I watch as Harriet gasps when she sees the heading.

"It says Florence Gibbs! Is that your proper name, Flo? Florence! Well, I never! So who's been writing to you?"

The best thing I can do is to act as if it is unimportant, for I want to be alone as I read the contents.

"I expect it is a just a letter of thanks from Her Ladyship for my work. That's the sort of thing they do. Don't fret, it won't be an order for me to return. Oh Harriet, you've done that very well!"

She holds up the shirt for me to see and my approving smile is the praise she needs to bolster her confidence. It's another small step towards normality and I find that very gratifying. Thomas has started to bang the table, so Harriet moves quickly to intervene by encouraging him to help her at the sink while she prepares vegetables for our meal tonight. With some hesitation I carefully open the envelope and start to read.

My dearest Florence,
It saddened me to hear of your family circumstances, but I fully understand the need for you to return home. I trust the future will be better

for you all.

I do so miss your strong presence and shall be forever grateful for your help. A pleasant girl called Jane Marsh has kindly taken your place for now, but if you should consider returning as my personal maid there will always be a position here for you.

Respectfully yours,
Caroline, Lady Gressingham

In folding the letter and tucking it inside the envelope I can at least feel a sense of satisfaction that I have done my best. I am very grateful for her kind words, but they fail to influence me or change my mind. Deep down I acknowledge that I shall never go back, for that part of my life is over. What cannot be taken from me are the wonderful memories I retain of those special outings when I was privileged to see different parts of our country. There will come a time when I feel able to tell my stories to the others, about the wonders of our towns and the beauty of the sea resorts, of travelling by steam train or riding along in a carriage. For now, all that will have to wait.

Chapter 42
Postscript

There is a welcome warmth in the air this morning as I gaze out from the kitchen door at the abundance of blossom upon our apple trees. That is a favourable sign, for it augers well for a good harvest later in the season. It pleases me for over the last three years I have profited well with my baking and have even acquired the affectionate name of 'The Pie Lady'. I shall always be grateful to Mrs Mason for her assistance and wise words. She has been a great help to us all. Naturally, it has also meant that her son is on hand to help us when things needed fixing, so it's not surprising that our relationship has strengthened. I start to blush for I can hear Bertie whistling as he strolls down his garden path and heads for our door.

"Good morning, my gorgeous flower!"

He stands with his hands on his hips and grins at me as if he knows a secret.

"They will be reading the first banns tomorrow at Sunday service, Flo. It'll be June before you know it and me and you will be wed."

Just the sound of those words sends a happy shiver through my body, but I grin and hang my head in embarrassment at the thought of really getting to know Bertie. He pulls a piece of paper from his top pocket.

"Your pa has found your birth certificate, so I'll be taking them up to the vestry later today. Better push off now, I've promised Father I would give a hand whitewashing the walls. Got to get it looking spick and span for the best little lady in the world!"

He blows me a kiss and returns to his cottage, his shock of ginger hair glistening in the morning sunlight. That brief mention of my father serves to remind me of the whole sad episode and I step back into the kitchen. Pa is changed in so many ways having suffered badly with bouts of sickness brought on by his heavy drinking. After one severe doctor's warning he did resolve to stop and to his credit he has never touched a drop of drink for the past year and a half. I think we all felt remorse that he had been shunned, but it was Harriet who insisted he was to come home. I think she is atoning for her own actions for she has made it her mission to make him feel part of the family again. We all keep an eye out to ensure he does not lapse into bad habits again. The biggest change we see is in Thomas, for he has responded so well under her care. He still tends his precious hens, but Harriet has encouraged him to help her with the gardening. The results of his early planting are showing already and it pleases us all to see how happy he is now with his efforts. I often wonder what Ma would think about us all, but I hope she would have been proud of all our achievements. My biggest regret is that she will not be here for my big day.

There is a clatter of feet coming down our stairs and Mary bursts into the room. She is growing taller by the day and seems to have boundless energy, forever rushing here and there.

"It will be all right if I go with Evie today? I promised and her mum said I can."

I have to remind myself they are off to the town market, but I do not pry because I rather guess she is on a search to buy a wedding gift for us. She impatiently tugs my arm.

"Oh, please say yes, Flo!"

"I hadn't forgotten, Mary, but just you be polite to Evie's mother. Go on, you rascal! Have fun."

She shrugs her shoulders in delight, kisses my cheek and rushes out, leaving an eerie silence until Lizzie too comes down.

"Is it just the two of us then? Have they all gone out this morning?"

There are times when I feel so thankful that Henry and Joe have steady work and are able to live out. Jack will be working today delivering groceries and Harriet has left with Tom to collect from the bakery. Pa has also gone out to help one of the villagers fix a fence.

"Now, big sister! We need to sort out what you are going to wear and now is as good a time as any. I was thinking you'd look lovely in that pretty lemon dress you were once given or will it be too small on you now? Why don't we go up and you can try it on!"

Dear sweet Lizzie, ever eager to make the most of what we have yet I already know that dress is far too tight to wear. I've only kept it as a reminder of the carefree times I spent with Ophelia. Perhaps it is time to pass it on to Mary for I'm sure she will be gladly accept the offer. Since my twenty-first birthday last week, I've been thinking long and hard about what I could possibly wear. That had been such a memorable day when I was crowned in the traditional way with a wreath of ivy and peony blossoms with all the family giving me their special cards. It felt very grown up knowing I was now an adult with a freedom to make my own decisions, but it was Albert who made the decision that night when he boldly stated he wanted to marry me. We had gone strolling and were caught up in a thunderstorm and had to race back. I must have looked a terrible sight with my wet hair, but he proposed on the doorstep and I fell into his damp arms with profuse acceptance. The speed at which he has organised the date has rather taken me aback, but I want our wedding to be as simple as possible in respect for the family finances. I know this is the time to tell Lizzie.

"Come on, then, you can help me. I've got something to show you!"

We race upstairs and Lizzie flings open the closet door, but looks puzzled as I get on my knees and feel towards the back.

As I pull out the bag I only hope the dress hasn't been spoiled and I hold my breath as I start to unroll it.

Lizzie stands with her mouth open wide in amazement.

"Oh Flo! Why have you kept it hidden away all this time? It's beautiful. Where did you get it from? Oh, do try it on!"

So many questions I don't feel able to answer truthfully as it inevitably brings back memories of my earlier life and what it might have been like had I stayed with Lady Caroline. I hurry to try it on, praying it will still fit me.

"It was a gift, Lizzie, but I always felt it was too grand to wear, especially when I returned home. Now I am having doubts and wonder if the colour is too dark for a happy occasion. What do you think?"

"Oh it's such a pretty pink. I think you will look just grand!"

We hear voices below signalling Harriet's return and I'm eager for her to voice an opinion, so I call her.

"We're up here Harriet. Something to show you!"

I can tell by the look on her face she is unsure of how to react.

"You look stunning, Flo. Are you planning to wear that for your wedding?"

Lizzie and I can sense she has some doubts, but we are delighted with the suggestion she then makes, for it seems an ideal solution.

"I've had a thought. Why don't I ask Sue if we can borrow the cream lace jacket she wore at her wedding? I think it would make her feel as if she was contributing something towards your marriage. It will look very elegant with the pink showing through. Oh Flo! You'll be a lovely bride!"

They help me take off the dress and then hang it safely on a hook so that the creases will fall out. Both girls then leave me to sort myself out and I hear them whispering as they go down. That gives me a warm feeling to know they are on hand and I can't believe how lucky we have been. I shall miss their jolly banter when I go, but I won't be far away! You see, the small one-bedroom cottage at the further end has been empty for two months since the death of Old John Groom and unknown to me, Bertie has taken on the tenancy on the condition that it gets painted and repaired. I couldn't believe the news when he told me, but it's a perfect solution. To think we'll be living nearby and just a few steps away from my current home… It will be ideal if I am still needed to help Pa, Tom or the girls.

There's one more thing I must do and that is to investigate the contents of the package given to me by Mrs Heath when I departed from Folkestone. It still lies tucked in my travel bag, but I do not think it will upset me now as I had once feared. It is smaller than I recalled and I can see my full name is written clearly on the front. The wrapping falls away to reveal a small ivory box containing a tiny brooch. It gives me a thrill for it is in the shape of a sea shell with a solitary pearl fixed in the centre. I can only guess it is given as a reminder of my time by the sea and now I feel foolish for having kept it this long and rather mortified I never corresponded with her. As I go to replace it, I spot a folded slip of paper in the box. The words written there throw all my previous sentiments away. My mind is in turmoil as I shamefully realise the gift is from Jean-Claude. Just the sight of his name evokes deep feelings that I thought long suppressed and I just stand there wondering if I am following the right course of action in marrying Bertie. A sudden shout from below alarms me and I guiltily shove the box into a drawer.

"You've got a visitor, Flo! A handsome young man to see you!"

I can hear Mary laughing and that sound is reassuring.

As I step into the room it appears quite crowded with everyone grinning as if they are keeping a secret. Lizzie speaks out.

"Albert's got something to tell you, Flo, or is it Florence?"

Now they are all giggling and I'm none the wiser. He comes over and escorts me to a chair before thrusting two certificates into my hands.

"I think you ought to be prepared to hear my full name for when the vicar calls it out and promise not to laugh!"

The girls are now laughing as I read aloud, "Albert Victor Gladstone Mason."

Lizzie shrieks out. "Now take a look at what you were baptised!"

I hardly dare look at my own birth certificate, but do so, and end up laughing with them. Apparently, I am named Florrie Victoria Gibbs. After all my grand illusions, I'm simply called Florrie.

Albert leans over me, his eyes twinkling as he grins. "But whatever you're called, you'll still be the girl for me!"

Looking up at all their happy faces, I feel humbled, but satisfied that I am back where I belong.